Catch Me

Love Thieves Book 1

By

Heather Long

Published by Decadent Publishing Company, LLC
Look for us online at:
www.decadentpublishing.com

~A Note from the Author~

In 2008, I had an idea for a story, a story about a Robin Hood-style thief, one who took from other thieves in order to return stolen history and precious items to their rightful owners. Over the years, tales of how many families lost valuable pieces to Nazi looting and how, even after the war, it was hard for those who survived their hell in the camps to locate much less receive back what had been theirs...those stories touched me. While no work of fiction can undo any of what has come before, I believe it's important to never forget.

The item stolen in this tale is not from one of those families, yet the thief who goes to reacquire it works for an organization which dedicates itself to the repatriation of art to where it belongs. Mingling the idea of doing the right thing with a legendary item which promises good fortune seemed like a fun idea then and remains so today.

After undergoing significant edits, I present to you the first of The Love Thieves trilogy: Catch Me. I hope you enjoy Max and Anya's tale as much as I did writing it.

Heather

The value of the Fortunate Buddha is not the precious stones or metals, but the legend of good luck it brought to the temple visitors who made a wish and a prayer while rubbing its ruby-studded belly.

Three things cannot be long hidden: the sun, the moon, and the truth. –

Buddha

Chapter One

The rope would hold. Her timing ran perfectly even under the clock for the bag, tag, and replace. High above, the ambassador's guests celebrated the New Year's Eve ball. Orchestra music penetrated the reinforced shaft walls. Hovering five feet above the pressure-sensitive floor of the ambassador's private vault, Anya Swift—recovery agent extraordinaire—flipped on the rope, tightening her abdominals so she hung upright rather than upside down.

The change in position made the ascent easier and reduced the chance of nausea. Excitement skittered through her belly as she shimmied up the rope. The sweet scent of the vanilla lotion she'd applied earlier mingled with the saltier tang of sweat.

Hush.

Never get too excited before a job finishes. Her butterflies would have to stay in their cocoons until the Fortunate Buddha could be returned to where he belonged. Five minutes before her absence at the party could become an issue. Clearing security as a disheveled guest might be overlooked; clearing security after a prolonged absence with a valuable stolen object in her possession invited trouble. One did not tempt the hands of fate, for fate possessed a mean right hook.

The weight of the idol pressed along her spine. Crafted of gold, the religious icon wore a ruby solitaire in its belly button. The value of the Fortunate Buddha lay not in precious stones or metals, but the legend of good luck it brought to temple visitors who prayed while rubbing its ruby-studded belly. True or not, her job meant retrieving the Buddha from the hands of the thieves who'd removed it from the Taiwanese temple.

I am so taking next week to spend time working on my tan.

The inane thought might seem out of place under more

ordinary circumstances, but the inane kept her sane. The strong, tensile cord coiled into a compartment in her belt as she ascended. If not for the sound sensors, she'd whistle.

I can work on my tan, eat at the cafes on St. Ville Riches, and maybe even read Mom's last manuscript. I told her I would read it last week, but it was Moscow and then Tel Aviv and then Morocco and, silly me, I left it at home. I am so....

The fuel spurring her absurd thoughts sputtered out on an empty tank of shock. Halfway up the shaft, strung between the hatch and a hard place, she stared right into the lens of a slender, flat cam pressed into the wall. Casual surveillance would call it a rivet in the structure, but, up close, the lens glowed with a faint red light.

An undocumented camera.

In the vault.

Staring right at her.

Anya considered her options. Slide down the rope and return the Buddha—accepting failure for her assignment—or continue up and leave the party as swiftly as possible. Her watch vibrated a warning. The loop on the security cameras lasted forty-five seconds. Not enough time to descend, replace, and ascend again.

The red light stared at her unblinkingly.

I am so screwed.

She could spare just five seconds for the mental debate. The memory of Max's familiar face drifted across her mind's eye. She'd seen him at the party earlier, but she came to Morocco for a job, not a flirt. Now she would have to combine both.

She continued her ascent, barely clearing the access hatch and closing it with the borrowed code before her watch signaled the loop ended. Every camera below recorded live once more.

Ready or not, Max. Here I come.

Max took another pass around the dance floor with Roberta, a woman who smelled too heavily of sweet caramel and summer apples. Worse, she wore the scent his mother favored, most likely purchased after researching him. He'd seen her too often at his parents' recent schedule of events to consider it a coincidence.

The scent transported him to his childhood, hot parties, uncomfortable suits and his mother's soft recriminations when he failed to behave. Fond memories, some of them, but hardly seductive, and he had no desire to associate them with this vapid partner. So, he kept his arms loose, but his frame locked, preventing the voluptuous breasts desperately trying to escape his partner's sequined V-neck from pressing against him.

"New York, London, and, of course, Milan. You have homes in all three, yes?"

"Hmm." The situation required only noncommittal answers.

"I thought so. I will be traveling with the show, but we are allowed additional days in each city as needed. The menswear debuts are always ahead of the ladies. I know the best designers, and I could help with any selection process."

Too conditioned to let his boredom hang on his sleeve, Max tilted his head to the side. The gesture urged her to continue.

"Of course, if fashion isn't what appeals to you, the parties are divine. Valentina throws a gala in New York and Milan, but she usually gives London a pass. The masquerade in Milan is the greatest event of the season. I think we could make a striking couple, my light to your dark; of course, we'd have to work on the color coordination. I do not look good in purples or greens, I prefer the deeper blues—a sea theme, it has appeal, yes? Like your home in Majorca?"

He nodded his head absently. Roberta's conversation weighed on him, as did her careless attempts to entice him with her lowered voice. Even with the wall of glass doors turned out to the crisp desert air beyond, the great ballroom combined a sultry mix of foreign dignitaries, under-dressed celebutantes, the bedazzled and over-pedigreed nobles, and just the right amount of nouveau riche. Not that he wasn't just as pedigreed as all the other bluebloods present, more so than some.

The corner of his mouth quirked upward. He wasn't sure how he let himself get dragged into these events. He spared a glance at his dance partner, who seemed to think she'd said something amusing. The first-born son of Lady Amanda Prentiss and French financier Jacques Sauvage, he was used to the insipid attempts to engage him on and off the dance floor. His partner continued to prattle on in bastardized French tinged heavy with a New England accent.

Then she appeared, her perfectly toned body sheathed in a black silk dress. He shut out the sound of his dance partner's voice and studied the captivating woman across the room. The slit in her dress played peek-a-boo with a length of bare, tanned leg. The red heels were nearly his undoing, a riot of color like a whisper of provocative promises.

Anya.

"Max?"

"Hmm?" A perfunctory response to her use of his name.

"You're not listening to me."

"I heard all about Milan, Paris, and New York. Fashion does not interest me, I'm afraid, chérie." High fashion certainly held no fascination for him, but his palms itched to follow the sway of Anya's hips beneath the sheath. The sheen of boredom dulling his evening ripped away, and victory dangled her like a succulent fruit, ripe for the plucking. His lips curled into a deeper smile as she hunted the room, passing him briefly before returning. The connection sizzled along his nerves.

He met her smoky gaze with frank appreciation and barely checked the urge to beckon the nymph in her sexy-as-sin black dress with tousled hair piled into an artful display. She looked like she'd just rolled out of bed. He nearly groaned at the image because he'd love to roll her right into that bed once more.

"Do you know her?" Roberta's tone climbed, a thin wire of high-pitched annoyance vibrating beneath the words.

"Our paths have crossed from time to time." She's the one who always gets away, the one who haunts my dreams.

"Time to time?" Roberta's nails dug into his shoulders, but he barely felt them. Only years of relentless drills about manners and decorum kept him from shrugging her off. "I think your eyes say much different."

"Roberta, you are a sweet woman when the mood strikes you, but let's not pretend it's more, hmm? Excusez moi, s'il vous plait," he murmured, releasing her and patting her hand before abandoning his dance partner without a backward glance.

Prague, Four Years Earlier

The meetings were dry, boring, and populated with one too many self-proclaimed security experts. Max wasn't even sure why he'd agreed to the meetings in the first place, except Pietr had volunteered him for the task.

Pietr, his cousin and a consummate troublemaker, had probably lost a bet and ponied Max up as a way of paying it off. After a long day of meetings, Prague's fogged-in airport had stranded him. A wide variety of foreigners populated the private lounge.

The Prague Conference involved a large number of security firms competing for bids at the best corporate computer security jobs. He had declined to bid on any one contract, a fact that failed to discourage any of the authors of the five thick proposals cluttering his briefcase. Corporate security never lacked for wordiness. He contemplated a second bourbon when the crowd thinned enough to reveal her, sitting at the other end of the bar. The black silk skirt hugged her curves when it wasn't parting to give him a wild glimpse of long legs.

Her body caught his attention, but the wide, full-lipped smile she bestowed on the bartender punched him in the solar plexus. As if aware of his scrutiny, she tossed a glance his way, one eyebrow lifting in inquiry.

It might not have been an invitation, but Max wasn't about to let the window of opportunity slide shut. He abandoned his perch to circle the bar, loosening his tie with one hand and wishing he'd dumped the briefcase with his pilot.

"Dobré odpoledne." He didn't let a little thing like broken Czech be a barrier to a beautiful woman.

"I'm sorry, I don't speak the language." Her low, throaty voice carried a distinctly American lilt.

He grinned. "May I buy you a drink?"

Anya resisted the urge to fidget. The ballroom population consisted of a cabal of fashion that belonged on The Bold and the Botoxed.

The last place she wanted to be.

Making it exactly where she needed to be. Her mother had often insisted on creating what she called plastic pearls of wisdom or as Anya dubbed them "playful platitudes" to placate the recalcitrant. Who knew Mom, the librarian, could get it so right?

Sorry, Mom, she offered up in silent apology. But I need the real thing at the moment, not the plastic kind.

Needing to keep it professional, she skimmed the room, seeking his very specific pair of forest-green eyes framed in lashes so thick the feminine part of her drooled with a touch of envy and, yes, a lot of lust. No matter how often Maxwell Sauvage frustrated her with his in-the-way attitude in the past, the delicious flutter quivering in her belly when she saw him was worth repeating.

Breathe, Anya. Breathe. The image of his mouth hovering over hers during the opening of the Paris gallery collection heated her blood. She'd been sent to reacquire a manuscript, and he'd wined her, dined her, and invited her to his Rue 69 apartment, but she'd declined.

Yes, she'd resisted the urge to go to his apartment. She'd fought the longing to strip him naked. She'd fled the pleasure in his arms because of a job. Her job. Her commitment. But a damn job, nonetheless.

Her assignment in Paris required focus on the task, not getting laid.

Hardest. Job. Ever.

Warm light spilled down from the crystal chandeliers sprinkled throughout the ballroom, highlighting hair so black it gleamed blue. An electric pulse zinged through her. Tingles started at her core and rippled out. His broad shoulders stretched the fabric on his expensive suit in all the right places. She recognized the lean, tapered length of his torso, the graceful way he held his companion, and the sheer, exotic beauty of his dancing. No man should be so beautiful.

The first time she'd seen him—Prague—had been four years before, in an airport lounge. Boredom had kissed his features, draining his vitality. On the lookout for a contact, not passion, she'd been captivated by something in his eyes when they'd shared a glance. Love at first sight didn't exist, but lust roared to life between them.

A distraction was the last thing she'd needed, and she shouldn't have made time for the small talk. Yet, watching interest flush his face with renewed life reminded her of a sunrise in the mountains. She hadn't been able to tear her gaze away.

Then or now.

Fixing a smile on her face, she walked toward him.

His seductive presence had proved a nuisance in previous cases. He'd nearly blocked her acquisition of a stolen manuscript just a few months before. During that case, she'd nearly succumbed to his charms completely, willingly forgoing the opportunity to re-acquire the work for the IAAR.

Looking down to see his wounded eyes watching her from below at the library haunted her. Even after scrambling out, she'd waited for the police to show up. She'd sweated the drive to Calais and the ferry ride to Dover.

Her image never appeared on Interpol's watch list.

Her cover hadn't been compromised.

Her potential heartbreaker became an unlikely hero.

Maxwell Sauvage could be her ticket out of this mess.

Prague, Four Years Earlier

"May I buy you a drink?" The man's voice beckoned to thoughts of sleepy sex.

"I'm fine, thank you." Anya nursed a club soda to maintain a personal fiction while she waited for Jorge to arrive. He was late. A simple drop, but Jorge didn't have the papers to carry the painting across borders. She did. Unfortunately, he was hours late with his check-in, and she didn't want to be tipsy when he finally showed up.

Disappointment flashed through his forest-green eyes, and she swallowed a smile. Sipping her drink, she scanned the lounge but saw no sign of Jorge. She flicked a look at the man in his five thousand dollar suit, tousled black hair, and rich French accent.

She should let him return to his own perch and bourbon. Dismiss him with a flirtatious smile and focus on the mission, but she patted the stool next to her. "You could give me some company and let me buy you a drink."

His head cocked to the side, the corner of his mouth tilting further. "I don't know if I can let a lady buy me a drink."

"First time for everything, no?"

Max couldn't believe his good fortune. She walked straight to him. The luck eluding him since Prague turned around. Everything about her said catch me if you can—except her eyes. They went to some unfathomable place that made him want to beg, borrow, or invent the key to reach.

She strolled through the crowd as if she owned it. He'd thought to go after her but stopped when her attention latched onto him. Her expression burned with.... Challenge? Desire? What? Something went on in her delicious mind, if only he knew what.

He tensed. *Did she discover the camera? Link it to me?* Every effort he'd used for tracking her before failed. For four months, he'd used his connections and accepted invitations he would normally have ignored. Tonight's gala in Rabat, Morocco, was not his first choice for New Year's Eve, but the ambassador's boast about his latest acquisition rang bells in Max's mind.

He'd gambled on the right lure.

It turned up pocket aces because she walked right toward him.

Double or nothing.

"Maxwell." The name slipped from her lips like a gift, and he tightened the mental reins on the lust flooding through him like a schoolboy at Eton presented with his first kiss.

"Anya." Good show, old man. The syllables of her name rolled off his tongue and sounded almost blasé.

Almost.

Her utterly kissable mouth curved upward into an enigmatic smile, the same smile she'd teased him with from across the room. The same air of mystery tormenting him after each near miss they'd shared over the last four years.

Her lips haunted him. Drew him in. Held him captive.

"Fancy meeting you here." Laughter threaded through her words, droll humor in light of the cliché.

"Would you care to dance?" He didn't wait for her to answer, sweeping her into his arms and turning her into the waltz, drifting along as though pulled by a current requiring two steps forward, one step back and to the side, turn, two steps forward. He could waltz in his sleep. Oblivious to the others in the ballroom, he focused on the simple elegance in his arms.

It took everything he had not to kiss her. "How are you?"

"Well. And you?"

"Also well. It is an unexpected delight to find you here."

"Is it?"

"No."

"So you're still looking for me?"

"Always." The fierceness in his declaration caught him off guard. Not now, he reminded himself. Calmly.

"I'm surprised you haven't given up yet."

"No, you're not." The deep gray of her eyes reminded him of storm clouds on the horizon, forbidding, arresting—begging a man to test his mettle against the flashes of lightening and the thunder. "You should know, chérie, I never give up."

Prague, Four Years Earlier

Laughter flared like lightning in her eyes. He leaned back, resting his ankle on his knee as the bartender brought them fresh drinks. "Where are you headed, Miss...?"

"Hmm. Two drinks, a loaf of hot bread, and some cheese doesn't give you name privileges."

"No? How disappointing. Would a meal and the promise of dessert do it?"

Her laughter warmed him the second time around.

"Yes, I rather like your tenacity." The Queen of England could not have given him a finer compliment. His chest puffed fractionally, a flood of masculine pride at the discovery his Siren found his determination attractive. "In fact, I was rather counting on it and you."

"Oh?" He turned her expertly, enjoying the way her slender body molded to his. He dipped his head down, scenting the intimacy between them, as the music seemed to fade.

"Let's do away with the games, hmm? You're after the same thing I am."

"I hope so." He grinned, shuttering the kick of irritation behind practiced manners. In Paris, just four months past, he'd believed they were after the same thing—mutual satisfaction to a mutual attraction—to his bitter disappointment. He did not like to assume anymore. He also didn't like how much she affected him while seemingly immune.

Her smile grew, sparking more emotion in her cloudy gaze he wanted to understand. Max pushed the feeling away. He didn't need to understand to enjoy her. He didn't need to understand to succeed. He didn't need to understand period—and better still if he didn't. Understanding led to an exploration of deeper feelings and the potential of commitment. Not knowing her hadn't prevented his fascination or how perilously close he was to falling in love with a woman who worked with an agenda, lived her life on the edge, and happened to be a high-class thief.

No, he didn't need to understand her.

No matter what he wanted.

"What did you have in mind?" He guarded the hope flaring inside, trying to ignore the way her body fit his or how the warmth of her touch singed his senses. The rich vanilla scent of her, orchids on a steamy tropical night, took him far away from the ballroom, responsibility, and regret.

"I need your help." Of all the words she could have uttered, those were the last he expected to hear. From the clench of her jaw and the tightening of her lips, it appeared no easier for her to say.

"Pour quoi?"

He maneuvered them away from the center of the dance floor and closer to the musicians. The music would blot out the sounds around them, giving them a modicum of privacy. He smoothed his hand over the softness of her dress, enjoying the way her muscles shifted and bunched as they danced. He searched her stormy eyes for a hint to what she wanted, but they held onto their secrets.

"You know I am in acquisitions." Her fingers toyed with the collar of his shirt, teasing at the ends of his hair, which he did his best to ignore. He sensed intense negotiations on the horizon.

"If, by acquisitions, you mean you are a thief, then, yes, I am aware." A brutal cut to the chase. The sudden dilation of her pupils warned him he'd scored a hit. "And you need my help? Again, I ask, why?"

A couple brushed too near them and she reacted, narrowing the gap until her body pressed firmly to his. He nearly groaned from the sheer agony of holding her so intimately yet feeling as though they were at arm's length.

"I seem to have...." She struggled with the words, and he waited patiently. In negotiations, it was important for the other party to make the first move, to lay her cards on the table. It gave one time to assess the situation, to counter the offer, and to make the most of the presented opportunity.

"I seem to be in the unique position of returning an item, rather than taking one." She'd chosen the words carefully. Too carefully. He turned each one over, trying to discern what meaning hid beneath.

"Tonight?" Stillness muffled his heart. He'd examined the ambassador's security personally, reviewing the protocols, the safeguards, and the alarms.

"Yes, it must be tonight."

Despite reluctance, intrigue pricked him. "What do you have to return, chérie?"

"Ahh, no." A smile turned those full lips upward, curving the corners into a delicious bow on an even more delicious package. "I need your agreement first."

"It is not good business to agree to terms when you are uncertain of what will be required of you." He inclined his head, dipping to murmur along the soft shell of her ear. "It is even less intelligent to make such an agreement with a thief if she wants you to commit an illegal act, vous comprenez?"

She canted her head, the piles of auburn hair falling in girlish ringlets around her face. The style emphasized the pixie shape of her cheeks and the exotic tilt of her eyes, most likely inherited from an Asian ancestor.

"I don't need you to help me commit an act." Her lips barely moved, yet he could hear every word. Her grasp of illicit and nefarious activities proved a seductive torment.

"Then be precise, chérie, so we may negotiate and satisfy your request." Urgency flooded through him, his trousers uncomfortable despite their custom fit. He ached to sweep her off the dance floor and into more private surroundings. Perhaps he was a fool, but he wanted to just say yes, no matter what she wanted. He'd do it, if only to stay in her orbit a while longer.

Yes. I'm a fool.

"I removed the Buddha from the vault. But I need to return it." Her smile flickered, a fraction of uncertainty echoing in her words.

"You what?" Why did the words startle him? She's a thief. I saw her take the manuscript. She's linked to the disappearance of so many other items. That's why I planted the flat cam, because it was just the thing to attract her. Score in one shot.

"I'm not going to say it again." Her sultry little laugh knocked over his objections.

"All right." He understood. He scouted their surroundings. Despite the number of couples on the dance floor, the music shifted to a slower moody piano piece. Tugging her more firmly against him, he enjoyed the supple feel of her warm softness relaxing into him. "You don't have to say it again. But if you want my help, I want something in return."

For a brief moment, he wondered at his words. Why would he challenge her? Wasn't this what he'd wanted all along? To have her come to him? To seek him out? Here she was...in his arms.

And he wanted to make a deal.

"I'm listening." Her voice, low and husky, shot him through with warmth. Their first regrettable tango in Paris ended when she walked away. He'd blamed her, blamed himself. He'd given her too much power. But this was a chance to explore the passion simmering beneath every word.

Her pupils remained dilated, and he could feel the rapid thrum of her heart pulsing under his fingers. He resisted the urge, barely, to stroke her nape. She was upset. Despite the glossy come-hither smiles, something had gotten to her. His resolve hardened. He would help her.

But it would be nice to get something in exchange.

"I'll help." He pressed a whisper of a kiss to her ear, longing to tug the lobe between his lips and tease the sensitive flesh. "You. Me. The beaches of Majorca. Sounds like an exchange."

Anya stiffened, her spine straightening, and anger seethed up from the depths of her hungry eyes. "Just to clarify, you want to exchange services?"

"Fair is fair." The words weren't him. But her reaction intrigued him. How far would she be willing to go? "We could even negotiate it down to twelve hours. Twelve hours of just you, me, and a bed and wherever that takes us."

"Thanks for your generous offer." Venom dripped off the words as she pressed a hand to his chest and pushed away from him. "But I don't prostitute myself. Good evening, Maxwell."

He let her go, watching her all but stomp off the dance floor despite never once slamming her feet down. A traitorous smile tugged at his lips. Thankfully, she didn't turn around to see it. She might be a thief, but she wasn't willing to bargain with her body.

He approved.

With every stride carrying her away from him, her hips rolled invitingly. Smoothing a hand over his tie, he pursued. He checked his craving. The image of her drenched in golden sunlight and surf on a beach left him hard and wanting.

First things first. She needs my help.

And, by God, she will have it.

"Arrogant son of a bitch." Anya spit the words onto the bar, irritation clacking in the shallow breaths between them. Why his offer surprised her, she didn't know, and she wasn't going to examine it too closely. The outrageously blatant suggestion, however, threw off her game, and, rather than fumble further, she'd abandoned the aforementioned son of a bitch on the dance floor.

"What can I get you for you, ma'am?" The bartender swiped a red cloth across the mahogany bar.

His calm motions swirled the cloth in a soothing, swishing motion over the wood in hypnotic circles. The placid smile on his too-perfect tanned face and full lips spoke of perfunctory sympathy, caution, and just a splash of rebuke for her decidedly un-ladylike behavior.

Go to hell.

Anya swallowed the scalding thought, sliding her tongue over her tempt-me-old-flame-berry-pink lips, while fighting the urge to sneer in frustration. The ripple effect took effort and control, both long practiced on people and in front of a mirror. The desultory dissatisfaction on her face gave way to the debutante pout. Walking away had probably been a mistake, but it wasn't in her to prostitute herself for a job. She wasn't sure what made her angrier—that he'd asked for her body or the fact she'd been tempted.

He always tempted her, and she always resisted. Her job was in the way. Work she would not compromise. Not for the first time, she regretted not meeting Max somewhere, some when else.

"White wine spritzer." The deep-throated baritone, dark and smoky like forty-year-old scotch stroked her senses. Excitement skittered through her, fanning the flames of her annoyance. She would not be turned on and pissed at him at the same time. The arm belonging to the owner of the voice appeared in the periphery of her vision, but she ignored him.

"Dirty martini." She slapped her order down in a brisk tone.

"White wine spritzer," the baritone repeated, slipping the order over hers along with a one hundred dollar bill.

"White wine spritzer, it is." The damn bartender grinned, all white teeth and tanned skin. Shark. Point to Max.

She spun on the bar stool, black dress falling open to reveal long, toned legs in a pair of almost-not-there red strappy heels. Using her body to distract him—she wasn't proud. Her tormentor studied her, wearing a dangerous smile that beckoned her, predator to predator.

"You left too soon." He pressed into her space, overpriced tuxedo hugging his body. His too-muscled, too-strong, and too-male-to-be-contained by the traditional black-and-white suit.

Damn, he looks good.

"No point in staying. The food is dry. The wine is expensive. The company is dreadful."

"Touché, chérie. I thought the evening just got started, and we have only a few hours left until midnight." His green eyes gleamed with a reflection of a dozen crystal chandeliers that filled the grand ballroom of the ambassador's mansion.

"Midnight?"

Her bare leg brushed the warm cloth of his pants. The contact burned along her calf, but she refused to jerk her leg away, even as the tingles raced up to her thighs and swirled in a vortex in the vicinity of her belly.

"Midnight, the New Year—out with the old, in with the new...." His breath puffed little circles of erotic heat on her flesh, a tide of goose bumps sprinting along the skin of her neck, shoulders, and following the plunging neckline to her cleavage.

"In that case, you should probably move along because you are definitely not the new." Anya made the mistake of flattening her hand to his chest, as though planning to push him away.

The pulse in his throat leapt, matching the pounding cadence beneath her palm. She would have slid her hand away, but, like a striking asp, he captured her in his larger grasp, holding her hand fast to him.

"You came to me, remember?" He kept her on edge, barely acknowledging the bartender's return with the flute of effervescent white wine. The thick length of his thigh rested solidly against her crossed legs as he trapped her hand beneath his. The sheer weight of him filled the air, blotting out the ballroom with its tinkling glasses, swishing gowns, well-mannered men, and murmurs of a dozen languages.

"You said no, remember?" Her heart rattled like a maraca shaken by a frenetic gypsy dancing under torchlight and weakened her challenge.

"Actually, I don't." Max brushed the knuckles of his free hand down the column of her throat, pausing to lay a finger to the pulse point just above her collarbone. The scents of chocolate, coffee, and male flooded her nostrils, boiling away good sense. "I told you your cost. One night with me, twelve hours, in my bed, at my whim, free to do whatever I wanted."

"You might as well have said no." She moistened her lips, tasting the warm glide of lipstick and a mistake. His dark gaze dropped, focusing on her mouth. His pupils flared, and the shivery slip of black dress with its almost non-existent back seemed to evaporate under the steam in his stare.

"Make me a counter offer," he invited, his knuckles continued their lazy strokes along the column of her throat. Her skin tightened, tingling in anticipation of where his fingers would go next. Her heart jumped and twisted, a fish on a line.

"You could have me owing you one." A weak attempt at wresting control as he toyed with the line.

"I'd rather have you under me and then over me." From any other man, the line would have been laughable, but he made it sound like a caress, the words gliding over her nipples—teasing, tormenting, tempting.

"Not an option."

"Why not?"

She had no easy answer for his question. If it weren't for the idol's weight burning a hole through her clutch purse, she'd have already drawn him off into some secluded corner where they could torture each other through their clothes. But she needed to return the idol. Dammit. Time ticked down and not just to the midnight celebration, but to whenever the film on the damnable flat cam would break. The tight security would tighten further.

Maybe if she'd just cut and run right after slipping out of the vault, but that hesitation had cost her, and the flat cam still held her image. She'd lost her exit the moment she hesitated. Her backup plan had failed when she broke protocol. Returning the Fortunate Buddha was far from ideal, but she could save her ass now and retrieve the statue another time.

"Because you're not my type." A terrible lie, and they both knew. Max flashed white teeth as a chuckle rumbled up through his chest, vibrating her hand.

Instead of responding, he retreated a step, taking his scorching connection with him. Before Anya could exhale a breath of relief, he tugged her along. He held her traitorous hand a willing captive. The strappy heels on her feet kept her at eye level with him. He drew her inexorably toward the grand gold-and-red parquet floor, gleaming under the thousands of incandescent lights above.

His fingers curled around her nape, cutting off her escape and drawing her into the sway of his body as he began to move to the music that filtered through her clogged ears. This close to him, she'd almost forgotten the presence of the musicians at one end of the dance floor with their myriad of strings, horns, and percussion.

He tugged at one curl, an almost boyish playfulness softening his hard features. As he stepped into the beat of the music, he guided her effortlessly. Where she was soft, and curved—he was tough and thick. The hint of muscle stretching the white shirt flattened her breasts as he closed out all the empty space between them. He continued to toy with her neck, finally sliding his hand down the expanse of bare skin in a trail of tingles until he rested his palm to the small of her back.

"I think you're mistaken about your type," he said into her hair. "But you're running out of time, and the gendarme does not take kindly to thieves here, even beautiful, sensuous American ones with a pair of fuck-me pumps and a body with promises of soft plunder."

"You say the sweetest things." Seductive, not sweet, and her reply tasted sour on the tongue. His scent overwhelmed and left her wanting to rub her body to his. She followed him, a slave girl desperate to be in his harem.

What the hell am I doing? Anya withdrew from the intimacy of the dance. She forced her attention away from him and scanned the over-pedigreed crowd in their clouds of thousand-dollar-an-ounce perfume. He sidestepped another couple, threading through the crowd with enviable ease.

He spun her, twirling, around his celestial body before dragging her in. With a brush of his lips, he tickled the skin just behind her ear. His breath stabbed at her, tiny hot lasers of pain and temptation.

"What are you doing?" she hissed, bound by the hard band of his arm around her and his fingers digging into the curve of her hip.

"Looking after you, gorgeous," he murmured, becoming damn near immovable as he studied the room behind her. She tried to catch his eye.

It was a mistake. Tipping her head, she exposed the long column of her throat. She'd forgone most jewels for the night, settling on an elegant but simple strand of low-quality but high-color diamonds. They possessed enough flash to be noticeable but not enough to be memorable. The choker enhanced her vulnerability, cupping in a V just below her pulse, which, even as she thought about it, began to pound like a drummer at a parade march.

His gaze roved over her face as though feasting on every nuance of expression. He nudged her chin with his own, bumping it gently. The smooth surface belied the hint of stubble raising goose bumps across her body like fans doing the wave at the Super Bowl.

When he pinned her under with one languorously devouring look, her traitorous nipples tightened, and she dug her fingers into his arm, nails raking through suit jacket and shirt to dig at the flesh beneath.

"I bet you're a screamer, too." His words trembled with a warm throaty quality, laughing between the syllables. The last warning he allowed before his face dipped toward hers, blotting out the light, the room, the sound of wine glasses, whispery accents, and even the swish of expensive silk.

His lips slanted across hers, tasting of impatience and demand. She opened her mouth to rebuff him, but the flavor of him stormed her senses as though he were the allied forces and she the beaches at Normandy. She swung her right hand up to slap him, but her fingers fisted into his hair instead, drawing him deeper into the kiss.

Anya strained against him, the words detailing his vile conception turning to ash under the fire of his passion. A flush of chillier air stole her breath even as his lips slid along hers. After a brief interlude, his tongue caressed the seam of her mouth—teasing, tasting, tempting, and finally withdrawing—the absence of him so much keener following the hint of invasion. She shuddered, the cold skating along her nerves. Blinking slowly, she tried to wrestle her traitorous response even as he leaned away and settled his weight to the door he'd just shut.

The closed door to what appeared to be a private room.

Son of a bitch.

"There's that beautiful temper. I thought you'd melted to a puddle of wax instead of tempestuous demon for a moment there." He grinned at her. Did he enjoy the way her hands clenched, the flush scalding her cheeks, or the fact she could barely control the grinding of her teeth?

"Go to hell, Max, and get out of my way." She drew erect and jutted her chin out. She understood arrogance, even if she didn't appreciate it in others. She met his challenge with rebellion, absolutely denying the wild, naked feeling their kiss exposed.

"I don't think so." Disappointment dimmed his smile but did little to detract from the chiseled jaw, achingly green eyes, and Roman nose. He was every bit the aristocrat the pretenders in the other room wanted to rub elbows with, as though they could absorb the blue blood through osmosis.

"Fine, I'll go out another way." She wanted a mirror. Her lips felt swollen, soft, and pouty. The last thing she wanted was to look how she felt even if her hormones raged on overdrive. Pivoting on one four-inch heel, she stumbled a half step and frowned. A nook boasted floor-to-ceiling mahogany bookshelves and a veritable cornucopia of red, black, and brown leather-bound law books. United States law books.

"What the hell?"

Max shrugged and slid his long, tapered hands into the pockets of his slacks. Still leaning on the door, he looked like he could be waiting on any corner of the world—save for his five thousand dollar tailored suit hugging every delicious muscle.

"The ambassador is fond of his eccentricities. The study of the American legal system is just one of them. But this room is meant for private study." He tapped the door with the heel of one shoe. "And soundproofed. It's also duller than dirt for most of the refined palates out there, so we have some quality time without anyone listening."

"Listening?"

"Can we call a moratorium to the games, Anya? Your Louis is out there."

Fuck! Louis is here? She didn't check the clutch purse in her hand. The weight of the idol dragged on her with every breath she inhaled. Fear pounded in her ears, the throbbing memory of betrayal and hate congealing her blood.

Her history with Louis du Monde, complicated by half-truths, innuendos, and outright deception, tightened the noose. She'd taken advantage of his interest in her to access a secure facility once. The man rarely forgot unfulfilled promises. Unlike Max, he never appeared amused or intrigued, only vengeful. He also had a reputation for being a thug with a pedigree. Blue blood didn't make his bite any less vicious. She really needed another way out of this room.

"Well...interesting."

"What?" She'd nearly forgotten her erstwhile captor and current obstacle.

"You're an amazingly adept liar. But I don't think you can fake the damsel in distress vibe without a grain or two of reality."

"I have no idea what you're talking about." She dismissed the cold fingers of unease probing along her spine.

He canted his head, his fathomless gaze boring into her. "You're not here with Louis."

Years of discipline and control couldn't arrest her flinch at his name.

"No, I'm not here with Louis." She studied the book-lined walls. She glanced upward. Air ducts fed into the room. She spotted the vent above one of the bookshelves.

She could make it, if she lost the shoes.

Three hundred dollar red satin Badgely Mischka pumps. Her inner Vidal cringed.

But she could do it.

"Is Louis looking for you?" His voice changed, the accent softening from the rolling syllables he favored when he spoke French to the harder, clipped vowels of his British upbringing.

"I really hope not. But whether he is or not, I would prefer he did not find me here." An understatement, but she gave up the charade of trying to seduce Max or letting him seduce her. She needed to move now. Returning the idol might not be an option. She needed to cut her losses and just go.

How did she get into this mess? Every encounter with Louis ended in disaster. Max's distaste for the man was the only reason she'd trotted the arrogant French count out as a distraction.

"Anya." He caught her arm, drawing her back to the present. "You were serious about wanting to return the idol earlier?"

"Yes."

"But you stole it."

She went silent. Let him think what he would. She couldn't reveal her purpose here any more than she could expect him to believe it. Her work with the International Art and Antiquities Recovery agency began with a binding contract. She'd agreed to follow their rules. They gave her all the excitement she could crave and an outlet for her impulses, but her parents had taught her never to make a promise she couldn't keep.

Honor should not come at so high a price.

But if it were easy, it wouldn't be honor, would it?

Raising her chin, she met his scrutiny, unflinching. "I will not sleep with you for your help."

He hissed out a breath between his teeth, frustration edging through the civil veneer he wore. "You are a vexing woman."

She shouldn't have smiled, but the way he said vexing made her belly flutter. Not the most obvious choice of words to hear from the man who danced with her, pursued her, and seemed very intent upon bedding her. She wasn't sure where his determination came from, and, right now, she didn't care.

Needing his help and a willingness to owe a favor differed from selling her body.

I'm not a whore.

When she would have spoken, he pressed a finger to her lips. The scent of his skin brought the simmering in her belly into full flame. Turning him down would be so much easier if he didn't turn her on, dammit. The way his finger brushed along her lip invited her to say yes to whatever he proposed.

Mistake!

Her inner voice shrieked. She liked to think of the sound as the conscience drilled into her by her very conservative parents. Her liberal attitudes and outlandish choices often left her Midwest parents at a loss.

"Truth?" Max spoke again, gritting the word out as though it cost him to say.

"All right. One truth."

"Do you really want to return the Buddha to the vault?" Why the hell else would she have approached him? Then again, he was here for the same reason as she. He wanted the statue. Right?

"Yes."

He went still. She tried to imagine the thoughts going through his mind. A muscle ticked in his jaw. A vein throbbed in his forehead. God he wore frustrated well.

Down girl, she reminded herself. Job first.

"All right. We will return the Buddha."

At what cost? "For?"

"Pardon?" He raised his brows.

"You'll help me for what?"

"It's free of charge, this time." The tension relaxed out of him, and she dug her fingernails into her palms to fight the urge to touch his soft smile. His thumb continued to glide over her lower lip.

He hypnotized her like this—watching her, relaxed and satisfied with the nebulous promise of pleasure.

"I don't think there will be a next time," she said, brushing the pad of his thumb with the tip of her tongue.

Her inner voice shrilled, and she could barely repress the groan, savoring the hint of salt and male.

"All in good time, chérie. Stay a moment. I will see if your Louis is...near." The way he said the words indicated a level of distaste she shared, but he took his hands away, leaving her strangely bereft.

Anya closed her eyes, and inhaled deeply. The vibrantly sexual and raw hint of his masculinity assaulted her senses. No one should smell so good.

Mistake!

"Oh shut it," she murmured to herself.

"Pardon?" He stood scant inches away from her, all sexy and tantalizing.

"Nothing. Is it clear?"

He went perfectly still and looked for the entire world like he would kiss her. If he did, she wasn't going to stop him this time. Her pulse raced in anticipation.

"Oui, chérie. It is clear. We shall return the idol." He took a half step back, puncturing the intimacy and offered her his arm.

Her anticipation for the kiss crashed. Fickle much? she demanded of herself. This was what she wanted. Return the Buddha. Get out of the pinch. Avoid losing her job, her credibility, and her freedom.

So, why the hell am I disappointed he capitulated so easily?

Chapter Two

Her disappointment surprised and pleased him.

He guided her out of the law library and through the heart of the ball. They'd only been sequestered for a few minutes, but he already resented the presence of so many people trying to steal his attention. Even the hungry Roberta followed in their wake, despite being attached to the second son of a Milan fashion house. He set a deliberate pace, weaving through the crowd, exchanging nods and pleasantries. More than one pair of male eyes settled on Anya in speculation. He understood the appeal of her swollen lips and tousled hair. Even her silk sheath suggested all manner of sin.

It took everything in him not to slip off his jacket and cover her. He fixed a hard stare on a wandering duke with speculation in his smile, turning the would-be poacher away. The man may be a philanderer, but he could point his philandering elsewhere.

Anya was taken.

Max cocked his head to watch her as they continued across the room. He wondered if she understood the seduction drifting like a lace train behind her. A part of him hoped she didn't. The minx distracted him enough. His only saving grace lay in her reaction, one indicating she wasn't immune.

A thrill of pure masculine satisfaction flooded him. Her eyes were heavy-lidded, and her cheeks were flushed. He put that look on her face. He made her feel that way.

Good.

"Something amuses you?" Her voice summoned him away from the image of peeling away the black satin sheathing her like a Christmas present begging to be unwrapped.

"Perhaps." They'd circumvented the dance floor, strolling

together as though they didn't have a ticking clock to beat. He could appreciate her attitude, but he would enjoy it more when they'd completed the task and he could dig deeper. He wanted to know her.

All of her.

As they stepped out through the double-wide glass doors onto the stone terrace, the chill of the night washed over her. He could almost see her nipples pearling under the sheath. He paused, slipping off his jacket and laying it over her shoulders.

"Better?"

"Yes, thank you." She watched him from beneath lowered lashes. Darkness shadowed her expression, but he imagined she remained as unfathomable outside as in. His body tightened, need thrumming through him. He wanted to see her wearing the same look and very little else.

He enjoyed the colder air. While it did little to cool his ardor, it cleared his mind. "Shall we walk?" He offered his arm again and enjoyed the feeling of her hand sliding along the crisp white shirt. Even through the fabric, he could feel the iciness in her slender, delicate fingers.

Why did this woman make him think of the fragile orchids his mother cultivated? A sensual flower needing copious amounts of care and tending or it withered and drooped. He cut the thoughts off and focused on the task.

"Of course." If she wondered at his words, she didn't show it. Instead, they walked the length of the stone terrace where a few couples stole away from the ballroom to cool off.

The last hour of the year counted down to midnight. Terraced with multiple gardens, the ambassador's home reflected the Burgundy region of France. A vineyard even peeked over a far hill, but the snow he would expect at home was strangely absent.

He knew the layout of the ambassador's home well. As they left the ballroom area, security tightened. The men patrolled the perimeter with deceptive languor. To the untrained, they were merely another set of partygoers drifting from one area of the party to another. But Max recognized them, and they him.

He turned her away from the terrace to re-enter the ambassador's home through another set of doors. One of the security guards started forward but retreated when Max shook his head. She slanted another look up at him from beneath those lashes, and he tightened his grip on her arm, keeping her with him.

Her lips parted in surprise, but he shifted, narrowing the

distance and pressing his lips to hers in a whisper of a kiss. "Play your part well, chérie. We need them to believe us." They needed to look like lovers escaping for an assignation. A vicious little thrill twisted inside of him when her face softened and she closed the last few millimeters separating them.

The flavor of raspberry cream tart exploded on his tongue as he traced her lips, folding her into his arms. Her slender body trembled. Could she be as overwhelmed by their connection as he? His fingers curled around her nape, clasping her to him as he ruthlessly delved into her mouth, his tongue slipping past her teeth to duel with hers.

Her low moan vibrated through their kiss as she acquiesced and he let go of the door to wrap his arm around her. His pants constricted against his cock. A small, unctuous little voice in the back of his mind reminded him of work to be done, but he slammed a mental door shut and contented himself with exploring her flavor.

He tasted of foreign spices, brandy, and raw male. She'd resisted the assault, but his whispered warning reminded her of the danger. The hell with it.

She didn't give a damn about her situation, not when he plundered her with a kiss as though he couldn't satiate his hunger. The flitting thought of security vanished, quickly followed by the idol, the ball, and even the little flat cam. She could only think about the vibrant taste of the man holding her and the hard length of his cock tenting his pants.

Dampness flooded through her, and the evidence of his arousal should have punched through her clouded thoughts. Wrong time. Wrong place. When his arm stole around her, she slid her hands up the crispness of his shirt. His heart thundered under her palms. Right man. When his tongue demanded entrance, she opened to him.

The moan vibrating her throat sounded alien. It didn't belong to her. It couldn't belong to her. *For the love of God, I'm supposed to be a professional.* His hands slid down to cup her bottom. She quaked with anticipation.

"Max." She could barely withdraw—her mouth moist from his, the flavor of him spearing on her tongue.

"Hmmm?"

"Buddha."

"He'll be there, chérie." His low-throated growl sent her pulse racing with wild promises. But she didn't want it to be there, in her purse. She wanted it back in the vault, far away from her. Who the hell has access to the damn flat cam?

For all she knew, her image could already be out on the wires to Interpol. The ambassador's security force hadn't scooped her up. Yet. The only relief she'd experienced since seeing the flat cam in the first place.

Job.

Have. To. Do. The. Job.

"Max."

He sighed, the warmth of his breath feathering along her cheek. She could wish the pressing weight of the Buddha wasn't clutched in her hand. More, she wished the tempo of his heart didn't tell her he shared her excitement.

She could wish for many things. But she needed to be practical right now.

"All right, luv, if you insist." He wasn't pleased. Even in the shadow of the terrace with the weak light cast by the torches placed for atmosphere, she could see the grim tightening of his jaw. He held her for another few seconds, as though wrestling with his own cravings before grabbing hold of the door, yanking it open, and all but thrusting her into the room beyond.

The first thing she saw was the bed. Really? She cast a questioning glance at him.

"Oh, I know, luv. I see it. But we'll be good as gold now." Desire erased the air of French sophistication. The Briticisms were the real him. The man she'd met in Prague and then Paris and even Florence. My Max.

Whoa! Shut up right now. He's not my anything.

She slipped his jacket off and passed it over to him after he closed the door. Keeping a firm grip on the clutch purse, she smoothed her dress and tried not to focus on how easily she had been ready to shed it.

Or how much she wanted to take it off.

Return the idol. Buy enough time to find where the flat cam transmitted. She might be able to call Hugh or Dante. They could figure out the signal. She could steal the tape.

But first, the evidence. The secured idol would alleviate any charges. She could bluff about her presence in the vault, but no missing idol meant no crime. She wouldn't have to worry about the local "gendarme" and any hefty prison sentence.

Even better, she wouldn't have to explain anything to her handler, Walter. A shiver raced over her skin. Walter wouldn't be forgiving. The IAAR worked too hard at their reputation with their clients and keeping a low profile everywhere else. She couldn't blow it. They didn't offer second chances. She didn't want to disappoint Walter, lose her job, or, worse, lose his confidence and trust.

Avert. Just don't even think about it.

"Anya?" Impatience dragged at her name. The kissing display had hopefully convinced the guards they'd stolen into the room for a more private encounter.

"Yes. I am ready."

He nodded and shut the curtains leisurely, even going so far as to lock the terrace door. He slipped the black jacket on and motioned to the inner door leading into the main house, stepping into the dimly lit hall where thick carpet muffled their progress along the white walls. The white walls boasted gold-filigreed moldings and heavy oak frames on the wall paintings, palatial and opulent without being a showstopper.

"The ambassador keeps private suites on the ground floor?" She kept her voice low, half-expecting someone to appear at either end of the secluded hallway.

A faint smile flirted with his lips. "Of course he does. This way." He motioned to the left and took a proprietary hold on her elbow to guide her down the hallway.

He moved with confidence and ease. If he weren't so contained, she'd almost liken his stride to a panther stalking his prize. Yet he maintained an air of aloofness with casual ease she envied. She needed to learn how to move as he did.

Hours spent in torturous study under a drillmaster who would make her repeat the same steps over and over again until she thought her brain would die from the sheer boredom of the repetitiveness. Yet the same training allowed her to shimmy up a rope, slide through an air duct and into an expensive dress to mingle with the elite as though she belonged. She was good. He was better.

Her chin came up at the wandering thoughts. She might not "belong" to their exclusive club with her solid middle class upbringing, but she'd certainly earned her right to be there. She caught Max studying her. Canting both eyebrows upward in query, she resisted the urge to scowl at his answering head shake. Whatever he thought, he wasn't sharing.

Perfectly fine by me. We've shared a little too much on this trip already. Their secluded hall ended at a T intersection, and he guided her left. He continued to walk with purpose, his loose stride accommodating the rolling hip walk her heels demanded.

A door opened ahead of them, and Anya found herself pushed to the wall, Max's body thrusting against her as his mouth closed on hers. She could barely swallow her groan at his swift possession. His tongue stroked inside, a master locksmith gaining entry.

Her fingers clutched at his suit jacket as his hands gripped her bottom and brought her hips more forcefully along the rigid length of his erection. Playacting or not for the benefit of the chuckling couple leaving them to their play, his hard cock stroked her sex through their clothes. A thrill fluttered wildly in her stomach.

The intruders moved along, but he refused to stop as he left her lips and traced the line of her jaw. When he brushed the pulse leaping just below her jaw, electricity surged through her. Her traitorous fingers wandered into his hair and luxuriated in the feel of its softness. She wondered at the contrast his silky hair and raspy morning stubble would make after a night of lovemaking.

His teeth grazed her earlobe. His hand slid over her hip, the heat of him penetrating the silk and satin, sending her up onto her tiptoes.

Warm male laughter vibrated next to her ear. "We need to get moving, luv."

He slowly withdrew and studied her with those too-damn-sexy green eyes, and she mewed.

Mewed. What the hell am I? A cat?

The sound mingled with his laughter and splashed icy reality onto her passion. Soft muscles stiffened. She uncurled the fingers from his hair and released his jacket. Embarrassment rushed to her cheeks, and she curled her lips in self-disgust.

Bad enough to be swept away, worse to be mortified. He smiled, slow, devastating, and far too appealing for words. Oh yes, he knew exactly what he did to her libido, and it pleased him.

Bastard.

"Shall we?" She choked the words out, barely recognizing the husky tone in her own voice. The sooner they put the idol back, the sooner she could put distance between the two of them.

Getting the hell away from him would be the best thing. Yes, absolutely the best thing.

Liar.

Shut up. You're not a coward or a slut.

If her internal conflict showed, he gave no sign of noticing. Instead, he ran his fingers up the side of her dress and carefully adjusted the top where her nipples all but peeked out.

They were hard and tight. Tingles radiated out from the light contact. The man seemed intent on killing her with need. She slapped his hands away and adjusted the top herself.

His devastatingly sexy smile turned to a full-blown grin.

The jerk's enjoying himself. And so was I, until he brought up the job.

Could one strangle the angelic inner dialogue serving as her voice of conscience? She imagined the devilish side of her skewering her conscience with the pitchfork.

Pfft, the inner voice mocked. That's not what you want to impale yourself on. Immediately, she glanced at his midsection and the outline of his cock straining the front of his tuxedo pants.

Her tongue flicked over her swollen lips, a thrill of satisfaction simmering in her blood.

He was aroused because of her.

Oh, yes. Nice symmetry.

"Anya." His sultry voice hovered right next to her again. "Changed your mind?"

"Nope." Liar.

"Pity." He slid his hand down her bare arm, cupping her elbow and tugging her to his side. They moved down the hallway. Lust pulsed with every beat of her heart. Willpower and training kept her on her feet as they walked down the long hallway toward the double doors at the end. The farther they went, the dimmer the lighting grew.

The dusky shadows were ideal for trysting, as evidenced by their moment against the wall and earlier on the patio.

And the dance floor.

And Paris.

And Bucharest.

Enough. Her frustration mounted. She was not some pimply-faced teenager who'd never been kissed.

Close enough.

She planned to personally pluck every downy white feather off her little angelic tormentor if it didn't shut up. Her conscience must have been paying attention to the seriousness of her threat because it finally acquiesced and silenced.

She blew out a long breath of relief and focused on her

surroundings. The painted white walls gave way to polished, golden-oak walls as thick carpet spilled over onto matching wooden floors with heavy rugs thrown everywhere.

For some reason, she expected the ambassador's private living quarters would have far more security with the huge ball going on in the east wing. Yet, even the atmosphere was hushed. Modern pieces of furniture were scattered amongst the weathered and well-loved antiques. A Queen Anne cabinet caught her eye, and she nearly drooled at the Louis the XIV Calais inlaid marble accent table sitting between two dusky-rose chairs.

Anya's palms itched as she drifted toward them. If they were imprinted correctly, it would mean the ambassador lounged in three-hundred-year-old chairs.

Max's fingers bit into her arm, tugging her away from the beautiful work of art with the newspaper lying on the seat as though left there after a quick scan.

She wanted to lounge in the chair, run her fingers over the soft wooden accents, and set a glass of wine on the expensive marble. He tugged again, and they left behind those treasures to see more mundane accents in the great open salon, which seemed to suggest the owners really lived within these rooms. A stack of knitting sat in a wicker basket at the end of a chaise lounge while family photographs of the ambassador, his wife, and presumably the rest of the family decorated the mantle.

She shook her head. She needed to clear out the lustful thoughts. With one last lingering glance at the priceless parlor, she fell into step with him. Her bare leg brushed his pant leg, and the hand on her elbow fell away as his arm stole around her to press her hip closer to his.

Pretty objects.

Pretty man.

Hmmmm. The angelic warning bells remained silent as she basked in the morass of want and need. On the far side of the salon, they entered an office filled with books, a mountain-sized desk, and a dozen more antiques—from the world map dating to the days of Columbus to an elegant globe occupying a space next to where the ambassador's laptop sat.

The vibrant contrast of old and new lifted her estimation of the ambassador. She could prowl around his private quarters for hours. Good thing she hadn't expected this level of luxury before committing to the job. Then again, if she'd known this when she'd planned the idol's retrieval, she would have made more than one contingency to pick out some of the heavier pieces.

Max strolled right through to a book-lined wall. It must be near the vault if she'd not misconstrued the direction they'd traveled through the house.

"Been here before, I would presume," she murmured, content to lean on him as he reached his hand up to the shelf and something clicked. The panel rolled aside. A secret door.

Of course.

The classics were the classics for a reason. Near-perfect construction hid the seam of the door until he'd pressed the release and revealed a plain, ordinary gray wall with a keypad and computer console.

"One moment, luv," he whispered, stealing another kiss and leaving the taste of him on her tongue as he pulled away to swipe a plain card along the top of the keyboard. The screen lit up as numbers danced across them. He typed in a series of ten digits then waited as the numbers continued to scroll.

A second swipe and the console buzzed. She frowned and glanced over her shoulder at the oak paneled door separating the office from the salon. The lack of security in the ambassador's quarters troubled her. She'd scanned the rooms on the way in and found, despite a plethora of cameras in the public areas, no evidence of video surveillance or electronic defense.

Very strange.

She frowned, considering the options and then glanced after Max. "Everything all right?"

She didn't like the high-tech stuff. She'd have preferred to descend via rope, but her window of opportunity was no longer available. The virus program had shut down the laser security in the air ducts for a short timeframe. Too short for her to just drop down and put the idol back in the first place.

Too late to deal with the flat cam.

Hard timing required dedicated and excellent planning, but it created problems, too.

"We're fine. Just a few more moments." He typed on the keyboard, and she twisted with indecision, torn between skimming the room and skimming Max. His forehead wrinkled in fierce concentration. His dark brows drew together. His parted lips moved in the silence, as though whispering encouragement to whatever his skillful fingers were trying to stroke out of the keyboard.

Closing her eyes, she tipped her chin up, mentally counting to ten. He typed on the keyboard. He didn't stroke the keys. He talked himself through the program. He wasn't seducing it with those magical lips.

Seriously, Anya? You got it bad.

For once, she didn't respond to the angelic voice's warning. After all, her conscience wasn't wrong. She counted her breaths.

One.

Two.

Three.

Her pulse refused to stop doing the samba. She inhaled deeply the decadent musk of crushed pine sharpening his masculine scent.

She didn't even bother counting as she drowned in his aroma and how much she wanted another taste of him. Yeah, her plan wasn't working either. She opened her eyes to see the door to the vault open and his amusement creasing his face.

She started forward and stopped when he held up his hand. Lifting her brows in question, she frowned when he rolled his hand over and beckoned with his fingers.

"The idol."

The hell he said.

"Anya." Warning slid under the syllables of her name. "We have two minutes. Hand me the idol. I will return it."

"How can I trust you?"

"You can't."

How...refreshing. She preferred the unexpectedly blunt response. The clutch purse seemed heavier, and she struggled with the questions warring in her brain. Caution said her task, her responsibility. Practicality argued in favor of getting his hands dirty. He wore no gloves; his fingerprints would be on the object, not hers.

'

"Ninety seconds, beautiful. Decide."

Stuck between a rock and a bomb shelter without a key. No more time for wimbling. She asked for his help, and he seemed prepared to deliver. Flipping the catch on the clutch purse, she opened it toward him.

He nodded slowly, accepting her offer. The squat little Buddha dated to the fourth century. But it was the Fortunate Buddha, rubbing his tummy promised great fortune.

Despite the brief amount of time she possessed the Buddha, a pang shivered in her belly as he vanished into the vault with her prize. Second-guessing her gut never proved wise, yet....

Her internal clock ticked down the time elapsed since he disappeared. She watched the door, barely registering the rest of the room.

"Forty-five seconds," she whispered.

She waited for Max.

Waited for him to put the Buddha back.

Waited for him to step from within the vault.

Holy crap. She waited for him to be safe.

Relentless tension coiled in her stomach, threatening the half-swallow of wine she'd taken earlier. Sweat beaded along her upper lip.

Twenty-five seconds.

The keypad he'd worked on began to blip from blue to red.

Twenty seconds.

The keypad emitted a beep.

Fifteen seconds.

A hushed roaring filled the silence between the beeps.

Ten seconds.

She took a step forward, lower lip caught in her teeth. She could barely make out syllables in the roaring.

Eight.

Another step forward, her heart thundered in time to the yelling of the crowd in the ballroom. The roar of three hundred guests penetrated even these dense walls.

Five.

The red light pulsed longer. The beeping became more strident.

Two.

Oh hell.

"Max...."

One.

He reappeared and the door of the vault slammed closed. His arms were around her. "Happy New Year, luv," he murmured before capturing her in a searing kiss. Desire raced along her nerves, pooling between her thighs until her pussy dampened.

Fireworks exploded beyond the great window, filling the night sky with glittering blues, yellows, reds, and purples painting the blackness in celebration. Her hands followed the hard muscles in his chest to twine her arms around his neck. He held her possessively against the rock-hard strength of his body. The rasp of his buttons over her silken sheath tormented her nipples to hard peaks aching for freedom.

Max broke the contact slowly, the fireworks display illuminating his face and granting his sexy expression a darker, sensual appearance. Her lips parted and her breath came in low, shallow pants. Her heart squeezed as he dipped closer, kissing the corner of her right eye and feathering a trail across to her left. He continued to rain those soft, gentle kisses down her cheeks, across her nose, and finally to her ear where he nuzzled the skin just below the lobe. Her pulse rocketed and boomed in her chest, matching the rockets blasting outside.

His murmured words thrummed through the haze of hunger, but before she could make out what he said, he swung her up into his arms and strode out of the room. His leashed passion simmered along her. His muscles barely strained with carrying her, and his lips never left her as he navigated across the salon and retreated up the illicitly hushed hallway to the terrace bedroom.

Shouldering the door open, he took her lips in another drugging kiss and kicked the door shut with one foot. He braced his shoulder against the wall supporting her as he plundered deeper with his tongue and the door's lock clicked.

Anya tried to see him, but the fireworks beyond gave the darkened room its only illumination. Each flash revealed the raw, naked need glittering in his eyes as he carried her toward the bed.

At the edge of the bed, he paused, his question obvious.

Yes or no?

They would never work. She needed to stay focused on the game, but there was too much history between them, too much longing, and she couldn't seem to stop thinking about him. He'd become an obsession. Obsessions destroyed. If ever there were a time to say no, she needed to act now.

"Anya."

Her sex clenched at the sound of her name on his lips. Her resistance clawed and melted at the demand present within the single word. Her body had absolutely no objections to what he wanted. Her thighs trembled, her skin grew hot and tight beneath his scrutiny, and she dropped the clutch purse. Cupping his face in her hands, she tugged him closer. He growled, and then they were on the bed, and he covered her body. Possession was nine-tenths of the law. In their case, Max seemed intent on making it 100 percent. Damn her if she didn't want him the same way.

Outside, the fireworks celebrating the New Year's arrival

continued to explode.

Chapter Three

Anya's drowsy, pleasure-drenched eyes captivated him. He stroked his thumb along the line of her cheek to the hollow of her jaw and the pulse leaping in her throat. He followed with his lips, hungering for another taste of her.

He traced a path to her collarbone and then along to the swell of breast peeking over the top of the dress. His tongue laved the tiny dot of a mole decorating the curve.

"Hmm, I love cherries," he murmured between nips and licks of her hot flesh.

Her fingers thrust into his hair, and she arched up to meet him. He traced the line of her nipple poking through the fabric, stabbing at him, begging. He took his time, sliding the hidden zipper on the side and peeling the fabric away. Fire kindled in her gaze, and her nostrils flared. Rising, he lifted her to let the dress fall away to pool at her feet.

His heart pounded.

The flickering lights from the fireworks outside continued to play over her smooth skin. She was perfect. She tanned topless. Continuing to explore her shape, he wanted to memorize every inch.

"You're beautiful," he whispered. Not for the first time, he wished he could read her, but the passion he saw smoldering in her expression suggested hidden fires burning out of control. He'd seen the dangerous blaze before, flaming just beneath the surface. He wanted to see it break free, igniting them both.

"You talk too much." The low, throaty tease stroked over him.

He stilled, her nipple caught between his thumb and forefinger. He watched her lips part and her breath catch as he rolled the tight little nub. "Oh? You like it quiet?"

"I like action." Her breath hitched as he grazed the sensitized bud with his fingernails. She gripped his shoulders and tugged invitingly. He dropped his head to lay a circuit of kisses around the hard beaded nub. A shuddering inhalation later, she sank her fingers into his hair, dragging him closer. He licked once, then twice, pausing to blow just the lightest whisper of air over the solid pebble of flesh.

She hissed. Yes, she liked the attention.

He chuckled and edged her torment further as he lavished her other breast with the same affection before sucking. He'd always tried to be a considerate lover, but her reactions were incredible. Max stole a look up at her face; the naked want in her expression fisted around his heart. This was the first real weakness she'd ever displayed. Drunk on the opportunity of her, all he could do was stare at her swollen breasts, the flush reddening her cheeks, and scent the sweet dampness of her arousal.

He'd wanted for her for so long.

Now she's mine....

Anya writhed, aching for him. The little voice in her mind shrieked mistake! But she ignored it as pleasure spiraled out from where he worshipped at her breasts. It was most definitely worshipping, too. None of her previous lovers achieved this connection when they touched her, stroked her, or tried to pleasure her.

They were all amateurs.

"You're still dressed." She struggled to touch him everywhere, from his hair to his shoulders. She wanted to feel the hot flesh the expensive cloth hid. When he levered himself upward, she murmured a protest until the jacket went flying and the shirt followed.

Bare-chested, he dove in for another kiss. She gripped his hair, and parted her lips for him, the fire in her belly spreading wildly through every limb. He kissed his way down her jaw to her breasts and then down the smooth planes of her stomach to her belly button.

Who knew it was an erogenous zone? She hissed out a breath as he continued to work his way along her body. His thumbs hooked into the scrap of black panties, and they went flying.

She gasped as his mouth traced the same path, tasting and nibbling along the soft flesh of her inner thigh. His fingers slid upward, brushing fire everywhere he touched until they glided between the damp lips of her pussy. Her body ramped up to the caress. When he grazed his teeth against the soft flesh where her leg joined her body, she bucked upward, demanding.

But he refused her, swirling his thumb around her clit in just barely there fashion, denying her the pleasure of the ultimate caress. A wild hunger, tasting far too much like need, roared through her. Breathless, she shifted to kick off her shoes, and his fingers bit into her flesh.

"No." He growled the order. "The shoes stay, luv."

Resistance roused inside her. She didn't like orders, but he pinched her nether lips, dragging a gasp from her. Fevered arousal followed the sting of pain.

"You will do what I tell you, right now." Raw need threaded through his words but did little to ease the force of his demand. He circled her swollen clit, vibrating pleasure through her. "Do you understand?"

"Max." She could barely form his name, so ravenous for him, it scared the hell out of her. All these years she'd dodged him, played games with him, goaded him, and fled before she could tie herself to him.

"Answer me." Steel laced the command in his voice.

"Yes."

"Good girl." He soothed a stroke across her clit until sensation drowned her. She forgot how to breathe. Dizziness swamped her; the rich masculine scent of him filled her nostrils. Her hips thrust up to meet him as he tormented her clit and then his fingers plunged into her. He slid along her body, his lips locking over a nipple, and he sucked hard.

Thought fled in favor of wild tingles radiating through her. She jerked, trying to force deeper contact. With a graze of his teeth, he nipped her—another sting of pain amping her pleasure.

"I'm going to fill you with every inch of my cock until all you can feel is me. You're going to surrender every ounce of your pleasure to me. You're going to let me play with your body until the only thought in your head is me. Do you understand?"

Oh my God.... Her professional intentions lay in tatters around her. His lips closed on her nipple again, sucking it so hard her back arched. She wanted to give him everything. He stripped her need bare, and his thumb traced a light cadence on her clit. She tried to flatten her heels against the bed, legs spread beneath him.

Begging.

But he still had his clothes on.

Desire blurred her resistance.

"Your sweet little pussy is going to clamp down on me while I fuck you with every push of my cock. You're going to scream my name as you come, but I won't stop...not even then."

He emphasized every word with the stroke of his fingers miming the motion of his cock. She gripped her thighs around his hand, but he was relentless. This was wrong—she should be running—but the thought jettisoned away as a million tingles cascaded through her. He was pushing her toward the precipice, racing her there faster and faster.

Euphoria swept over her, a fireball of an orgasm on the edge of detonating, but instead of pushing her over, Max withdrew, leaving her wet and gasping.

"No...." The word spilled out of her before she could stop it.

"Stay."

Was he serious? His flared nostrils, and taut lines around his mouth revealed he wanted her as badly as she did him, but he slid off the bed, leaving her naked, wet, and wanting. Her shaky little gasps of breath stripped her of her bravado. His hands went to his belt. She couldn't look away as he removed his clothes, revealing corded muscle, stiff nipples, and a lean, defined abdomen.

"Don't."

The warning stilled her hands. She'd been about to touch herself, and she hadn't even realized she'd moved. She fisted the bed's covering, watching as he discarded his briefs and freed his cock. The thick length of it jutted upward to his belly. The glistening head shimmered in the flashes of light from outside.

He's beautiful....

A masculine aphrodisiac, perfect and hypnotic. He stared at her as he drew a condom from his wallet, and she nearly wept as he smoothed it along the length of him. Her palms itched with the craving to stroke it into place.

"Do you want me?"

Her mind tripped at the stupid question. "What?"

One hand running over his sheathed cock, he stared at her. Tension flexed his jaw. "Do you want me?"

"Is that a trick question?" Her thighs clenched. He unraveled her focus, stealing into her soul and leaving her defenseless.

"It's a question you need to answer."

Her spirit rebelled, but her body pleaded. Their gazes clashed, but the blue flame in his darkened with demand.

"Yes. I want you." The admission fell from her freely. It cost her nothing. She'd wanted him for years, thought about him when she shouldn't. Allowed her lust for him to cloud her judgment, distract her from the job, and tonight....

Tonight, I used the feeblest excuse to get to you.

Shock rippled through her. She was woman enough to accept her blame. She could have gotten the hell out of there, but she she'd seen him in the party. Seen him and wanted him. Apprehension gave way to surrender and had the moment she approached him.

No, I surrendered the moment I entered the party. I could have just left.

He smiled, lunging forward, and slid his hard cock into her. Her breath caught as he shoved into the hot well of her sex. The agonizingly slow thrust left her sputtering with a pleasure so sharp it pummeled her regrets into half-forgotten memories.

Her back bowed as she arched, aching for more of him. He withdrew only to thrust deeper. Her nails dug into his shoulders where the muscles bunched with strain. He murmured as he kissed her again and then took her hard and hot. Each stroke brought her nearer to the precipice. The damn man drove her to the edge and then drew away once more.

"Say my name," he whispered from the near dark, his voice drenched in passion.

"Max."

"Yes, I like it when you call me that, chérie...." He filled her with a jerk of his hips, and she gasped.

"Max."

"Again."

"Max."

With every aching drive, she repeated his name. A litany to passion as every nerve ending in her body exploded in a wave of violent sensations rending her apart. She screamed his name as he drove into her over and over, just as he'd promised. His shout joined hers as he soared over with her. He collapsed on top of her, buried to the hilt. Heart thundering, she trembled with pleasure. Somewhere, the little voice of her conscience had been completely gagged by her recitation of his name.

He buried his face in the crook of her neck, tender, soft kisses brushing the flesh there. She should get up, put her clothes on, and get out. Instead, she slid the heel of one red shoe up the side of his leg, carefully so as not to hurt him.

His groan against her throat became a growl. Lifting his head, he stared down at her, and her stomach jumped as a renewed wave of wantonness struck.

"I told you, chérie. I love these shoes." The French was back.

"You can keep them if you love them so much." She trembled with the aftershocks, already imagining the hard cock driving into her again.

He chuckled and traced her cheekbone with his finger. "I'd rather just keep what's in the shoes, pet."

When she would have refuted him, he silenced her with another kiss, swallowing her argument. She was no one's pet, least of all his, but when his mouth and hands began to move, she forgot how to think, and then he swept her over the edge of passion again, touching, tasting, biting, tempting, until she lay boneless next to him, his hand curled over her hip.

She sighed. She needed to dredge up the energy to escape his delicious body and their hedonistic interlude. They weren't even in the bed. Instead, they'd simply fallen on top of it while taking each other.

His hand came up to cup her breast, possessive and gentle. A faint smile tugged at her lips. She loved this part—the time after the explosions of passion, just the two people wrapped in a blanket of intimacy. But did she really have the time to indulge herself?

The flight left in—she turned her wrist to look at the slender gold watch she wore—five hours. She still needed to retreat to the hotel, fetch her things, and notify Walter of the problem with the flat cam.

She would ask for a computer virus to be uploaded to erase all the tapes and, hopefully, destroy any footage before anyone could identify her. If it didn't, what would they find but her presence within the vault? Nothing missing.

They'd returned the idol.

A knock jerked her out of her reverie and roused Max from slumber. Ha, he'd fallen asleep. It was so wonderfully masculine. He'd pleasured her and then dozed, snuggled to her, his hands resting on her as though she belonged to him and he to her. Either way, his unexpected sweetness pleased her soul.

Of course, their uninvited visitor admitting himself could be bad news.

Max uttered an oath and shifted, jerking the coverlet up to hide her and blocking the rest of her from view with his body. She appreciated the light spilling over him to highlight the hard rope of muscle comprising his arms and stretching across his back. If he didn't work out regularly, she'd give away her jewel collection. He was in top form, crisp and trim without being over muscled.

"What is it?" he demanded.

"Your pardon, Monsieur Sauvage, but the ambassador asked if I could fetch you for drinks with the festivities winding down." Ahh, a butler or valet of some sort. He certainly had the sneer down in his tone of voice. Max didn't move, but she could see the muscle working in his jaw. He had no interest in joining their host for drinks, but it would be impolitic to turn him down.

"Thank you," he said stiffly. "Tell His Excellency I will join him directly."

"Of course, monsieur. Shall I send a...car for the lady?"

"Oh, the lady is just fine," she called out. "You just run along like a good boy."

Dismissed, the man shut the door, and Anya giggled when Max glowered down at her, although his expression softened at her laughter. "I suppose it would be too much to ask you be right here when I return, hmm?" He twisted to brush her cheek with his knuckles.

"Oh, yeah. Sorry." She couldn't shake the silly grin. The more she looked at him, the more she felt like smiling. "I have places to go, things to do, people to see."

His eyes narrowed on the last.

"Male people?" His voice dropped an octave.

Jealous, Max? "And if they are?"

"You could join me." The terse and gruff invitation didn't excite her, particularly not with the ambassador involved. Going unnoticed didn't happen in a diplomatic audience.

"Sorry. But I have to go. I'm leaving Morocco tonight." Why the hell did I just tell him?

He frowned. "Where are you traveling?"

"Now, that would be telling." She pushed herself upward, letting the hastily drawn up sheets fall away. His attention dropped to her breasts, and his hand stretched out, but she pushed it away and rolled off the other side of the bed. Not a shy person on the best of days, it unnerved her the way his gaze followed her toward the dress pooled on the floor. A quick glance around didn't show any signs of her panties.

Oh, well, it wouldn't be the first time she left a job commando, although the pleasant aching in her body and between her legs reminded her this was definitely the first time she left so satisfied and empty-handed.

"Anya." He caught her, drawing her back into his orbit. Electricity sizzled through her where their bare bodies made contact. "I can make the drink with the ambassador a short one, thirty minutes. Can you give me thirty?"

"Max, I need to go. I still don't know who saw me." She didn't want to bring up the camera.

"Merde, it doesn't matter. The Fortunate Buddha is in the vault. There is nothing for you to worry about."

"Except for the fact I went into a highly secure area, and, even if I didn't steal anything, it would still be breaking and entering. Go have your drinks with the ambassador, and thanks for tonight." With a glance to the bed, she smiled. "All of it."

"Fine, I will meet you at your hotel. Where are you staying?" He released her as she twisted away to slide into her dress.

"It doesn't matter. You should get dressed before the ambassador takes offense at your tardiness."

She slipped into the dress, wiggling her hips to shimmy the fabric into place. Max merely stood and stared at her, a muscle ticking in his jaw again.

He stepped toward her, and she held the dress to her breasts with one hand and warded him off with the other. "No, sir. You. Pants. Now." She kicked the tuxedo trousers toward him, and he caught them in one hand, still advancing at her.

Her mouth went dry. Gorgeous, sexy, long, lean, and hard. Not enough words to describe him. If he pounced, she'd surrender without much of a fight, but another knock at the door won the argument for her.

"Monsieur Sauvage?" The sycophantic little voice reminded him the ambassador waited.

"Dammit." He swore and dressed with barely restrained fury. She watched him, siding with silence as the better part of valor for the moment. She slid the zipper up, securing the dress with a small hint of regret.

A glance at a mirror showed her auburn hair coming out of the piled ringlets she'd shoved it into earlier. Rather than continue to fight with it, she released the pin holding the mass in an updo and shook out the length. The wild tumble fell midway to the center of her back, and Max made a harsh, choked sound.

Glancing at him, she smiled. Her hair surprised him?

"It's all mine, I assure you." She smiled, bending to retrieve her clutch from the floor. A hard arm snaked around her waist as he captured her. His hand tangled in her hair and turned her face to meet his lips for a kiss. One filled with a raw intensity and thrill, as though he was determined to imprint himself.

As if she could forget.

When he finally released her, she swayed on her feet. She knew if her lips hadn't been swollen before, they were now, and it took everything in her to not lunge forward and drag him to the bed with her. Again.

"Thirty minutes, chérie."

"I am at the Hilton. Room 634. I'll be there for three more hours."

What am I doing?

"The Hilton," he repeated slowly, as though savoring the greatest gift. "Room 634. For three more hours."

"For three more hours."

He looked at his watch and then captured her face in his hands, pulling her to him for another long, soul-searing kiss. "I'll be there in thirty minutes. Less."

"All right." She tugged at her lower lip with her teeth, savoring the feel of him. "I'll see you then."

The little man knocked again, and Max glared at the door. Fortunately, he didn't possess laser vision or the little man would be dead.

Anya stared as the door closed behind Max, and sighed.

I am so going to regret this.

"Yes," she told the room quietly. "I know. But God what a great mistake."

Chapter Four

R esisting the urge to bang her head, she stared at her empty hotel room. The cool air teased her overheated skin. Relief mingled with apprehension as she tossed the clutch aside. She climbed on the bed and reached for the vent above. Three twists with her fingernail, and the loosely attached cover popped off.

She rose on tiptoe and slid her hand into the cool air rushing from the open duct. The cell phone tucked right where she left it. After securing the cover back into place, she dropped to sit, dress spilling open on the side. The protected satellite phone required a code to turn it on, a code to dial, and a sequence to connect.

Finger combing through the tousled mess of her hair, she didn't fight her thoughts wandering to Max. Her body still ached for him. She should have taken off after they got the idol into place. Why on earth had she let him cart her to a bedroom?

"Station one," an impersonal voice answered, intruding on her rumination.

"Two-one-seven Sierra Delta Charlie requesting access."

"Stand by."

The phone cycled through a series of clicks as the call routed appropriately. Sliding off the bed, she tugged the side zipper down and let the dress fall off as she walked into the bathroom.

"Juliet?"

"Yes."

"Report." Despite the cultivated softness in his voice, Walter's tone resonated pure steel.

"Failure to retrieve."

Silence.

"Were you compromised?"

45

Sucking in a deep breath, she flattened a hand above her stomach, hoping to quell the butterflies doing jumping jacks. "Uncertain."

"Unacceptable."

"I know."

"Details."

"An undocumented flat cam recorded five meters above the objective." She crossed her fingers. "Retrieval was compromised."

"Understood. The flat cam wasn't in the profile?"

"No, sir. I disabled the others per protocol, but sixty seconds was up and no time to disable the flat cam. I also didn't have the equipment on site to handle it."

"All right." Walter's unflappable tone chilled the air. He didn't mince words, and he didn't use more than he needed. "You're on the next flight out. We'll work on contingencies."

"Yes, sir." Thank God for Walter. He was the IAAR to her and her highest level of contact. She knew there were other handlers and directors, but Walter was her go-to guy. He gave her the jobs, the orders, the schematics, and, when necessary, gave her hell.

The one she wanted to impress.

"Juliet...."

"Sir?"

"When did you notice the flat cam? You had a straight jump descent." There he is. Walter didn't miss a trick when it came to profiles.

"On exit, sir."

"So, you didn't see the flat cam until it already recorded you."

"Yes, sir."

"Go dark." The call clicked off abruptly.

"Nice talking to you, too." She sighed. Flipping the phone closed, she rolled her thumb across the latch, popped it open, and yanked out the SIM card. She discarded the phone into the trash and flushed the microchip down the toilet.

Go dark.

No contact. No calls. Go home. Use the alternate travel route. If she ran into any other problems...well, she was on her own.

The price of doing business.

Shower.

Shower. Then pack. It would give Max time to get there.

If he comes....

"Seriously," she told her reflection. "If you have a better plan, share it or shut it." She turned away to lean on the counter. Anya scrubbed at her face and shoved away. Fatigue should swamp her. Instead, all she experienced was exhilaration. She needed a shower. God love the Hilton shower. No matter what country she visited, the bathrooms were awesome.

The steady pulse of hot water saturated her, plastering hair to skin and massaging soreness in her muscles. The door to the hall thumped quietly. She'd locked the bathroom door. She paused, listening for the footsteps, then watched as the bathroom door clicked twice before opening.

"Beautiful surprise, luv." His voice drifted through the steam.

"I locked the door." Her heart sped up, a mixture of fight and flight. What the hell. She smiled.

He came.

"I thought you invited me." Warm honey slid through his words.

She listened to the rustling of motion on the other side of the curtain. A thump of shoes hitting the floor sent anticipation rippling through her belly. The rasp of his belt, and she shuddered.

"How were drinks with the ambassador?" She exhaled the words slowly, enjoying the pleasurable ache listening to him evoked. She soaped her hair with a citrus-scented shampoo, curiously comfortable with his presence. After all, he'd told her he came here to see her. Her go-bag packed and ready, she could have picked up the secure phone and been in and out in five minutes.

Instead, she'd lingered.

She'd waited.

Waited for him.

"Boring and long."

"Awww, poor little rich boy. You had to mingle with the elite." She loved the plaintive note in his voice and the sense of longing it struck within her.

Running her fingers through her saturated hair, she rinsed the soap free. The curtain jerked aside, and Max joined her in the steamy, tropical shower. Drinking in the long hard lines of his body, she smiled. The tapered waist, the broad shoulders, and the sprigs of dark hair curling deliciously over muscle definition earned through sweat and hard work. Damn, she was hungry for him all over again, and, God bless him, he already wore a condom.

She licked her lips.

"Hello, pet." He breathed out the endearment as his body framed hers and pushed her back against the cool tile. Shivers rippled over her skin, tightening her over-sensitized nipples.

"You trade endearments...luv, chérie...pet. Are you French or British?"

Instead of answering her, he slid his hands over her contours, shaping her breasts and her hips. He closed his fingers over her rear and lifted her, sliding deep in one thrusting move.

She tilted her head, the hot spray of the shower kissing her skin as his cock thrust deeper into her. He kissed along her jaw then down along the exposed column of her throat. Her pulse jumped at the touch, and she wrapped her legs around his hips, squeezing for balance over the slippery wetness, but he gave away none of the control.

He withdrew slowly, only to impale her deep. He kept the pace, smothering her questions in demanding passion as she thrashed with need. Saying nothing, he increased his pace pushing her to the edge, over and over. Tears escaped her as she clamped down on him until she exploded over the edge.

He returned to the bed, a white towel slung around his hips as though in decadent homage to his physique. With a small smile, he carried the room service tray. "Fresh fruit for the lady."

"Thank you, but I have to get dressed soon."

"Let's not talk about that right now." The bed dipped as he sat, then he slid the tray onto the comforter. She sprawled on her stomach, one foot in the air. Her body hummed from the lovemaking in the shower then the floor and, finally, the bed. The man's stamina should be bronzed.

She wanted nothing more than to collapse, snuggled to him, and sleep. But her plane would be boarding in—she glanced at the clock on the nightstand—ninety minutes. She would have to be at the airport to make it before Walter cut her off.

Focusing on Max as he filled two flute glasses with champagne, she chewed on regret. He'd ordered champagne, brioche, strawberries, and a dozen different types of exotic melons and cheeses. Pure decadence. No matter how much she wanted to stay, she needed to go.

On the job, her life wasn't her own. She answered to Walter and the International Art and Antiquities Recovery Agency. Even though Walter had ordered her dark, as long as nothing broke with regard to her activities, he would—could—capture her if she bolted or went off book. Their relationship worked when everything went as expected and she caught her plane on time.

"What are you thinking about?" Max handed her a champagne glass and bent to steal a kiss. Although, since she'd long since thrown the vault doors wide, he was more than welcome to loot all the kisses he might want to from her.

"Just enjoying the view. I have to admit, this particular Hilton seems to improve with every visit." She grinned and plucked a ripe strawberry from the dish. Her stomach growled. She'd skipped dinner to get into position in the air ducts before the party.

"I shall fill out a compliment card for you, then." He stretched out next to her.

"I don't understand you." It bothered her. The little niggling doubts, the questions, and the curiously quiet voice of reason and conscience shut up from the moment he took possession of her body in the shower.

"What's to understand?" He watched her over the rim of his glass, his dark-green eyes even more vivid in the less plush surroundings of the hotel. Two perfectly cut gems, flawless and inviting.

"Why did you help me?"

"Why did you ask?"

"Do you always answer a question with another question?"

He grinned. "Do you?"

She laughed, and his smile grew wider. His infectious charm, ease of laughter, and relaxation with the hustle and bustle of the world charmed her. He never hurried. He never rushed.

Why should he?

As blue-blooded as they came, Max was a third cousin to the Queen of England and related to four other monarchies through various marriages in his family tree. His father was a member of the elite. Not that he needed a title.

She'd seen pictures of both the Lady Prentiss and her husband through the years in the society pages, and if he aged half as well as his father...well, he would be even more of a catch. "I asked first."

"You did." He nodded.

"And?" Exasperating man.

"You did," he repeated, picking up a plump strawberry between his thumb and forefinger and holding it to her lips invitingly.

She took a bite, the fruit exploding with a mixture of tart and sweet on her tongue. She chased it with the champagne, the smooth, chilled liquid bubbling against her throat.

"You asked me for help." His smile devastated her willpower. As if the strawberries and champagne weren't enough. He added some cheese to a cracker and lifted it to her lips. "Why did you ask?"

The creamy cheese offered just the right amount of bite to underscore the strawberry's earlier sweetness. She rubbed her tongue against her teeth, mulling his answer and his question. "You have made a habit of being where I have been lately. I thought you might be in a position to help."

"Hmm...there's some truth there, but it's not why you asked me."

She delayed her answer with another swallow of champagne and stretched her foot, running her toes along the soft curls of hair on his leg. Heat from his shower-warmed flesh radiated across the bed like a drop of sunlight splashed against the sheets.

"Do you remember Florence?"

His expression tightened, and his eyes smoldered, amusement flickering in their depths. "I do. You teased me unmercifully and left me desperate and frustrated."

"Well." It was Anya's turn to smile, and she hid the grin of pure satisfaction at the admission gave her with another sip of champagne. The bubbly went straight to her head. "I didn't mean to leave you frustrated, although I do admit to a certain amount of foreplay over dinner."

"Foreplay?" He laughed, such a deep-throated barking laugh, it brought another smile to her face. "You danced like we were making love, you ate like you were licking your way up my skin, and all I could think about as you sampled those strawberries is what else I'd like you to do with your tongue."

The flush suffusing her wasn't only from her sated passion rousing at his words. She could feel the blush staining her face, and she tore her focus from his sinful lips to pluck another strawberry.

"Do you want an apology?"

"Absolutely not." He caught her chin in his hand and nudged her gaze up to his. "You made me ache with want, and I wanted. I wanted and I watched and I waited. But three months is a long time, chérie, to torment a man."

"It wasn't on purpose."

"Non?"

"Non." She kissed his fingertips. "Tonight wasn't planned either."

"Je sais que c'est vrai." He stroked his thumb along her lower lip. "Yet, here we are, and I should be satisfied with the having of you, and yet already I ache to have you again."

"This is a bad thing?"

"If you miss your plane, it could be a very bad thing for you, though I will not mind if you do."

Anya sighed and glanced at the clock. She agreed, it would be a very bad thing for her to miss her plane, but she couldn't deny she wanted to stay, too.

"You have not answered my question, chérie. Why did you come to me tonight? You came into the ballroom, searching for me specifically."

Truth?

Hello, little voice, where are you? Truth? Of course, her conscience went silent, leaving her to spin out here on her own.

"Yes, I knew you would be there. I saw your name on the lists of invited guests, and you were photographed in Rabat the night before. I believe she was a redhead."

"Ahh, Monique."

A rush of anger kindled at the name.

"She is a sweet girl. We dined at Peu de Fleur." Indulgent humor flooded his tone.

The anger turned to quiet rage as she considered the image from memory. Monique dripped in jewels. Perhaps Anya would relieve her of those burdens.

"You look so fierce, chérie. Jealous?" His mocking might have been playful, but her irritation ratcheted up another notch. Stretching to put her champagne glass on the footboard, she began to roll off the bed only to find herself pinned beneath him.

"You have nothing to fear from Monique. She is a friend of a friend, here on a modeling contract, and I promised to take her to dinner. Nothing happened between us."

"So?"

"So, you looked angry, and I didn't want you to think you needed to act on your temper."

"Arrogant much?" She lifted her brows, intimately aware of his thickening cock.

"So, you weren't jealous?"

"Maybe a little."

He chuckled and captured her for another kiss. Their lovemaking slowed but filled with more intensity as they explored each other's bodies. The man's fingers were little musicians of pleasure, playing her body like a well-honed instrument. When they were spent, she lay there staring at the ceiling, his arm around her waist, the gesture equal parts sweet and possessive.

She turned her head to the clock. Just under fifty minutes and, as reluctant as she was to go, she needed to slip away and dress. His expression relaxed in sleep. The lines furrowing his brow earlier when she'd approached him on the dance floor, smoothed.

She'd gone to Max because she'd known he would help her. She'd known it because he'd seen her in that gallery in Florence and he hadn't turned her in. Maybe a delusion, maybe wishful thinking, but he'd had plenty of opportunity to turn her over to the authorities, and she was still free. Six months before, a patron of the arts in Italy had announced the resurfacing of a lost work of art by Leonardo da Vinci. Speculation ran rampant about the painting with collectors flying in from around the world.

There on an IAAR directive, she went after the so-called lost painting. The work of art was lost for nearly sixty-five years after a Nazi SS officer collected it during a raid in Baldin, Germany, from a Jewish banker named Ernst Stauflman. Stauflman inherited the painting from his family; a gift from da Vinci to his many times removed grandmother for services rendered.

The family heirloom, like so many others belonging to the Jewish populations of Germany and their occupied territories, had been stolen. The Italian collector was the grandson of an SS officer. Whether he knew the true origins of the painting or not, the man refused all entreaties from the Stauflman family to return the painting.

So, the IAAR dispatched her to authenticate and retrieve. She'd enjoyed an evening with Max, dancing, dining, and talking. She'd enjoyed it almost too much. Their third such encounter in four years and he always seemed to enjoy pursuing her. She'd been reluctant to say good-bye, finally telling herself she could see him after the job finished. She'd even promised to meet him in a couple of hours.

At the gallery, when she'd looked down from her rope to see him watching her, recognition flaring in his eyes, she'd realized her work with the IAAR could have been compromised. It should have been compromised. She'd fled the country and left the painting with a liaison for safe return to the family. For the next few weeks, she'd studied the blogs and newspaper reports. Nothing appeared about the retrieval or her part in it.

She brushed her knuckles down his stubbled cheek and smiled

at him. The tenderness swelling around her heart had to be gratitude. Gratitude he'd not turned her in then. Gratitude he'd saved her tonight. Gratitude she experienced because, even after their various couplings, he'd demanded no answers about the Fortunate Buddha or the lost da Vinci.

"Thank you, Max." She brushed a kiss to his slumbering face and then forced herself to walk away before regret could bind her any tighter.

Tiptoeing around eggshells of longing and self-reproach, she slipped into her clothes and grabbed her go bag. She hesitated at the door. He lay sprawled like a dark god on the sumptuous white sheets, the disheveled bed and discarded strawberries a testament to their passionate interlude.

Walk out the door.

She gripped the door handle and whispered. "Maybe next time."

And then she left.

Max sighed and scrubbed a hand over his face. He'd known she would slip away. He'd hoped for otherwise, admittedly, but he'd seen it in her face each time she'd glanced at the clock. He'd used sex to distract her, but, once they'd sated those urges, he'd seen her focus return to the clock.

Dammit. He shouldn't have gone to sleep.

He rarely slept with a woman. He'd take them to bed, hold them till they slept, and then leave before they roused. It kept them from getting ideas about his intentions.

So, he took a thief to bed, and what did he do? Of course, he fell asleep with the hope she would be there in the morning.

He scowled.

"Anya.... Anya what?" He swore again. He knew her first name, but not her last. He picked up the phone and then dropped it. He would go to the manager and bribe the hotel booking out of him. He wanted her full name. He dressed and searched the room but found only those impersonal items provided by the hotel along with a disposable and non-working cell phone in the bathroom trash.

He paused next to the shower and inhaled the wonderful citrusy scent she'd washed her hair in the night before. He didn't know if she favored the oranges and night jasmine regularly, but he'd always associate the scent with her.

Frustrated, he finished dressing and shoved the tuxedo tie into his pocket.

He'd get more details from the hotel manager.
Or heads would roll.

***

Anya waited, restless, for the plane to land as it circled for approach at Heathrow. She'd arrived at the Rabat airport to find out her tickets had changed from Singapore to London. Images of Max assaulted her every time she tried to sleep on the long flight home. Not even the novel she'd picked up at the airport distracted her. She found herself wondering what he'd thought when he woke up.

Is he looking for me? Will he look for me?

Time to stop thinking about it. Not thinking about him meant thinking about the IAAR and Walter. Her reluctance to confront him.

Walter wasn't happy with the turn of events in Rabat. He was right to be unhappy. Still, for six years, she'd been an excellent retrieval agent. Leaving him little to complain about.

Except my attitude.

My need to take risks.

My rebellious nature.

Well, except for those things. She almost laughed at the matron-like murmuring of her conscience. The little voice in her head seemed to have regained her tongue once she left the hotel—and Max. She was all of those things. She liked to test her limits.

Her parents worked as a schoolteacher and a librarian in DeSmet, Minnesota. They'd lived in the same two-story blue house with white trim all her life. They were as ordinary as a scoop of vanilla ice cream. Nothing wrong with ordinary, but they lived their lives in a sort of regimental routine which left Anya screaming to get out by the time she turned thirteen years old.

She'd gained a lust for books and devoured them from a very early age. She loved the adventure stories. The tales of the women who left home to explore the world, from the frontier bride who would travel into the untamed west, to the pirate queens, and more. For a long time, she'd fancied herself one of those girls.

At sixteen, she'd started saving every penny she earned from various odd jobs. She'd packed her bags and hopped a plane the day after high school graduation. She'd promised her parents she would return for college, but after backpacking through Europe and picking up trinkets here or there, she'd discovered a gift for "reallocating" items from those who owned them.

"Thank you, ladies and gentleman, for flying with British Airways. We are on final approach to London Heathrow, local temperature is twelve degrees, and it is just after noon local time...." the pilot continued, offering informative tips on connecting flights, and she blocked him out.

She'd encountered Walter on her first big job.

Or the heist that went all wrong.

He'd pinched her on her way out, art in hand. Seeing only a one-way ticket to prison, she leapt at the offer Walter made her.

She had been barely nineteen and full of herself, but he'd scared the hell out of her. He was older, experienced, and possessed a ruthless gleam. Sometimes his attitude didn't match his age, or maybe it was the other way around. A dangerous man for certain...one she didn't willingly cross. Not anymore.

He'd given her a choice: take a probationary position with the IAAR or find herself handed over to the Belgian authorities. She'd never regretted her choice. The International Art and Antiquities Recovery Agency remained hush-hush and maintained private funding, but they sent her to college, trained her, and honed her skills.

She'd spent her first year on research and reconnaissance while she went to school. She'd acted as backup to other agents during her second, running point or tail to cover if need be. By year three and ten credits shy of a bachelor's degree in art history, she ran point on her own operations.

She'd also met Max.

All thoughts led to Max it would seem. She grimaced as the wheels bounced once upon touching down.

Need to get over my obsession. We had a night of pleasure. You enjoyed yourself. End. Of. Story. She sighed and waited for the plane to taxi to the gate. She preferred the happily ever after.

But your life isn't a book.

She sighed again. No, her life wasn't a book.

Just an hour outside of London, the IAAR headquarters occupied a manor house, which had reportedly served as the home to a mistress of King Henry VIII. Following conventional Tudor fashion, it offered the resplendent and the restrained. The great wrought iron gates were a work of art, depicting galloping horses. White stone walls soared alongside, creating a formidable barrier warning the casual visitor to stay away.

The guardhouse sitting just outside the gates served as a more forceful reminder, but for those who could press on past these warnings, the armed guard and the gatekeeper couldn't be bought. She let the rented Citroen idle while the guard checked her credentials.

Even agents were to be verified and then double verified. No one entered IAAR headquarters without the express permission of the sitting board members. While the IAAR's exclusivity made it private, they'd developed a reputation in certain circles, a mystique—their very own Internet legend. Recovery agents were disavowed in all cases, even those who came into the business from those certain circles and some went rogue on their own.

Not that it really mattered—if someone wasn't invited, he or she didn't get in.

The guard returned to the driver's side window and handed over her passport and identification cards.

"Mr. Reynolds wishes you to meet him in the garden. Tea will be served promptly at two."

So, she had thirty minutes to wash up and change before confronting Walter.

"Thank you, Charles." The older man nodded before resuming his station. A few seconds later, the great gates opened with a silence belying their size.

***

"Romanov," Max muttered, disgusted with himself for letting her slip away without learning her full name. He shook his head and looked across the table to his cousin, Pietr Sauvage. Dark-haired and eyed like his Russian mother, Pietr had inherited his strong jaw and noble bearing from his French viscount father, Max's uncle. Although Max contributed the crooked nose to his cousin's looks, the cousins shared few other features, and few remembered they were cousins.

The confusion served their relationship well.

"Anya Romanov does seem unlikely. You are sure the name the manager gave you is correct?"

"I paid him fifty thousand euros for the information. He wasn't lying." He drank a swallow of Turkish coffee. The cousins were sitting in a quiet coffee house on a side street in Rabat. Max itched to be moving, but he wasn't sure where he needed to be going. No sense in getting on a plane for Italy if she headed to the States.

Her American accent was unmistakable.

He considered her voice, her intonations, and her choice of language for a moment—American, but not from the Eastern cities. Somewhere in the west he would imagine but not the south. She spoke with neither the hard syllables he associated with those from the East coast or Mid-Atlantic States. Nor did she drawl as many from the South did.

He could see her in California.

On a beach.

In a bikini.

His body hardened at the mental imagery.

"Maxwell," Pietr sighed. "What is your obsession with the little thief? You prevented her from taking the Fortunate Buddha. You did your job. You maintained the integrity of the ambassador's security. Call it a job well done and move on. I know a fabulous cabaret that's just opened in Monte Carlo. We could be there tonight."

"I'll pass. Thank you, though." He took a deeper swallow of the bitter coffee and pondered his obsession. He'd been desperate for the minx. The elusive promise of catching and bedding the one who slipped away from him had driven him for months.

He hardly had trouble filling his bed, so the novelty of her refusal to just fall into line must have been what intrigued him.

So, what's my excuse now?

"What else could the manager tell you?"

"She arrived a week ago. She pre-paid the room. She checked in as Anya Romanov. She did not leave her passport at the desk."

"Unusual."

"Not if she paid ahead. There would be no reason to keep it for security." Max rubbed his jaw. The memory of her soft sighs and even softer skin filled his mind and left him harder and more wanting than before he'd taken her.

Ridiculous.

Possessing her should have eased the need, not increased it. But did I really possess her?

He paused to consider the possibility. They'd had sex, several times. At the ambassador's house, in her hotel room shower, on the counter, on the floor, and the bed at least twice.

As marathons go, he'd never been able to top three times in one night since his days at Cambridge. That he'd stirred so forcefully, so many times in as many hours, suggested his wanting went deeper.

He shied away from where the thought led.

No, he'd shared her body, not possessed her.

If he'd possessed her, she wouldn't have been gone with the dawn.

"You're wandering again," Pietr complained. "Did she order from room service? The shops? Anything local to suggest an interest or a hobby?"

"No. The manager actually remarked upon her behavior. She ordered nothing. She ate away from the hotel. She kept odd hours, coming and going without a pattern."

"Smart if someone is looking for her or looking for a pattern."

"Bloody brilliant, if you ask me." Not that Pietr had.

Despite his ire at her disappearance and his frustration at the lack of information to be found about her, he definitely admired his little thief for her intelligence and cunning.

"What about the ambassador's guest list?"

Max frowned. "What about it?"

His cousin sighed, a patient sound reminding Max of their parents. "Is Anya Romanov on the list?"

"No. I have a couple of people going over it now and identifying each of the guests."

"Any surveillance footage?"

He paused.

The flat cam.

Bloody tosser. He sighed at his own obliviousness. "She avoided the cameras in the main salon and ballroom. She always kept her back to them. But we may have another opportunity."

"Brilliant. Now, we shall collect the image and send it off for identification, and you can treat me to the casinos in Monte Carlo for my clever suggestion."

Max laughed. Pietr loved the part of the dilettante, despite the fact he was more devoted to his causes and obsessions than Max.

"Fair enough, Cousin. You can arrange for the jet. I'll meet you at the airport lounge in a couple of hours." He stood, leaving a few bills on the table. Far too much for coffee. But he enjoyed the little shop and the family who ran it.

And he always showed appreciation for the people and the things he enjoyed.

Chapter Five

"I'm sorry, Walter. Maybe I did handle it wrong, and, if I did, then I regret it. But everything in me said return the idol. Minimize the collateral and abandon the mission objectives to recoup another day."

"Instinct. What did your training tell you to do?" Walter sat across from her. Though she suspected his looks were misleading, his salt-and-pepper hair combined with a broad and flat face boasted a Native American tribe or three in his pedigree. His eyes were older, they'd seen everything, and yet...she'd never shaken the suspicion of something more to him than she'd seen.

He'd been her handler for six years. He knew her.

Too well, most of the time.

She couldn't lie to him.

"Training would suggest I could have secured my objectives more creatively."

"So you reacted rather than acted." A sigh layered through his words. "Disappointing. But it can't be helped now. What's done is done. The ambassador is scheduled to take a trip to Brazil in a few months. We'll work it out."

And I'm out...I lost it. I lost the Fortunate Buddha. Walter would hand the assignment to another operative. Her assignments were often confined to Europe, North Africa, and the Mediterranean. "Do you have anything else for me?"

"No. You can stand down. In fact, you will be on stand down until we see if there is any fallout from the flat cam." His final and immutable word sealed her future. If she stood down, she would stay there.

"What about research?"

"No, Anya. I want you to disengage fully. We need to be able to

59

evaluate threat level, if any. I won't have the IAAR compromised or tainted by association."

The words stung. She frowned and moistened her lips. There was enough money in the bank to cover any significant downtime. But what the hell am I supposed to do in the meanwhile?

"Are you making this leave terminal?"

"If necessary, yes. But I don't feel we are at such a critical point. Do you?"

"No, sir." Her perfunctory response lacked conviction. She shook off the doldrums and jerked her gaze upward to meet his. "No, I do not believe we have reached the point of no return."

"Excellent. Now, finish your tea and eat something before Brighid scolds us both."

"Yes, sir." She reached for a scone obediently. Walter refilled her teacup, and her mind wandered to the flat cam. Downtime. She didn't need downtime. She needed the video footage. She needed to know who took the video footage, who monitored it, and what they planned to do with it. Either would help her plan her next move.

Just because she couldn't work for the IAAR on a project didn't mean she would do nothing. She smiled as she added a dollop of jam to the scone. The hunt for her elusive voyeur could be fun.

Speculation filtered through Walter's sober expression, but Anya ignored it. He'd told her to stand down from new assignments, but he hadn't specifically ordered her to not investigate her problem.

Good as getting permission, in my book.

"What do you mean it's gone?" Pietr's voice crackled on the other end of the cell phone. Max paced the ambassador's terrace, confidant in the scrambler they'd designed to ensure the security of such phone calls.

"I scanned the tapes from last night's events. The digital and the standard—she did an expert job on looping his cameras." His chest puffed with pride for her work. If he hadn't known what she must have done, he really wouldn't have noticed it. In fact, without a pixel-by-pixel breakdown, it was likely to remain unnoticed. Her impressive skill made his second discovery all the more worrisome. "But the Buddha, the flat cam, and all the recordings are all gone."

"Could she have returned for it this morning?" Ever reasonable was Pietr.

Max raked a hand through his hair. "I don't know. But if she retrieved the discs, why did she go to the trouble of returning the

Fortunate Buddha only to take it again?"

"How do you know she didn't? Did you authenticate?"

"I don't have to." He'd replaced the duplicate with the original himself. She'd stayed outside of the vault while he'd gone in. No way had she slipped around him and the tag he'd placed on the original for verification.

It wasn't a con job.

"You're sure she didn't simply do an elegant swap, giving you the duplicate? Meaning she never entered the vault and there never was a digital recording?"

"She's hardly a femme fatale." The idea had occurred to him. But he'd reviewed their actions the night before closely. She'd simply had no time.

"Then I have no answers for you, Maxwell. Talk to the ambassador's head of security. Perhaps they retrieved the data discs for storage or some other form of protocol."

"How do you retrieve something you don't know is there?"

"You spy on the spy and take it from them when they are occupied with seduction."

"If someone took it, then they have Anya on the disc. She wanted my help to stay out of trouble."

"And now the little thief may be in over her head. Call it good riddance to elegant rubbish and let's head to Monte Carlo."

He slowed his pacing and studied the gardens. "No. Pietr, find her. Check the cities I gave you and the dates. See if you can find any other Anyas staying at hotels." He paused. "Check the Hiltons first." She seemed to favor the hotel chain. They'd dined at one previously, and she'd murmured something about their showers.

"All right. You are a terrible cousin to torture me with the promise of Monte Carlo only to steal it away for some elusive phantom."

"Pietr, just find her. I will make it up to you."

"Oui, Cousin, you absolutely will make it up to me."

He rang off and shook his head. Pietr would find something to torture him with.

"Monsieur Sauvage." The valet stepped out onto the terrace. The same valet who'd summoned him last evening. "The ambassador will see you now."

"Merci." Max glanced at his wristwatch. The ambassador would get fifteen minutes and not a moment longer.

"I could find no listing for an Anya anyone flying out of Rabat yesterday." Pietr sat across the broad oak desk. His hair disheveled, as though he'd been raking his fingers through it, and the stubble on his face suggested he'd endeavored heartily on Max's behalf. "The name, although not uncommon, was curiously absent from the ticketing charts I received."

"Are you sure they were accurate?" He growled the words, his mood growing grimmer by the hour. She didn't simply walk out of the hotel to evaporate into the ether. She'd gone somewhere. She'd caught a flight.

Hadn't she?

Max had taken the first commercial flight to Paris, leaving his jet behind at Pietr's disposal. His cousin arrived and came straight to the office from the airport. "Considering what you paid for the information." Pietr shrugged. "I am certain it was correct. After all, the man had nothing to lose in giving me the information I wanted and a reward if he pointed me in the correct direction."

"Then I've lost her."

"You sound forlorn." His cousin flashed a grin. "For a man who is expert in matters of security, you did not protect your heart well."

He simply glared at him.

"And now you wish to take it out on me, the messenger, tsk." Pietr spread his hands wide, innocence radiating from every gesture. "Perhaps I should refrain from sharing any more information. If bad news leads you to want to strike me, good news may encourage despicable things we should not countenance as cousins."

"Pietr." Max gritted his teeth. His cousin seemed to be having way too much fun at his expense. Pietr saw simple joy in everything, whether seducing a woman, stealing a business deal, disposing of a rival, or needling his cousin.

"I am a simple man, Cousin. I require simple things."

"You can have the house in Tuscany."

"Well, in that case...there were five flights departing at 7 a.m. Three international flights, one to Tangiers, and the final to Casablanca." Pietr paused, eyeing his empty tumbler with a hint of dismay.

Hissing a breath through his teeth, he stood and retrieved Pietr's glass. "Allow me to refill this for you so you might continue." He crossed to the bar and added three cubes of ice, a splash of gin and vermouth. Max preferred the straightforwardness of Scotch, but, at eleven in the morning, he would satisfy himself with coffee.

Pietr grinned. "Thank you. Now, as I said earlier, there were no Anyas on any flights out of Rabat. But there were three leaving Casablanca."

He went still.

"Ahh, you now appreciate your cousin more, no?"

"No. Any way of identifying the three who departed Casablanca?"

"Non, I simply left it and brought the jet to Paris since your search bored me."

Max ignored the sally and returned to his chair. Agitation vibrated through every muscle. It took physical effort to sit. He took a swallow of the black coffee, not even tasting it while he waited. Pietr knew more and he would spit it, or his teeth, out any moment.

"You are a lost cause, Cousin. A lost cause." Pietr tossed back the drink before setting the glass, ice clinking, onto the desk. "Three Anyas were booked on flights; only one actually left on a flight from Casablanca. It flew directly to Nice before continuing to London Heathrow."

"She went to England."

"Oui."

"What name did she travel under?"

"Anya Lund. She flew under a Norwegian passport."

"Lund."

"Oui. From the film, Casablanca."

"So she traveled as Anya Romanov in Rabat and Anya Lund on the flight out." He drummed his fingers. "I have another job for you, Pietr."

"I somehow suspected as much. You wish me to see what names she used during your previous encounters."

"Oui." Max smiled tightly, teeth gritting together. He had clues to her now. The use of historical names from film was a good catch. Romanov could have been a nod to the Russian grand duchess, or it could have been chosen from the multiple films about her.

"I will need specific dates and places and as much information as you can provide. And you will continue to owe me. I am beginning to think you're firstborn, for you do so abuse our family connection."

"Merci."

"De rien." He rose and took Max's hand in his own, shaking it firmly. "You fly to London, then?"

"Oui. I need to find her. It will take me a couple of hours to make arrangements. If you need the jet, simply send for it. Or we can rent another. I will want it at my disposal should we get a line on where she has gone."

"You are going to extreme lengths to find this woman. Has Cupid loosed his bow and filled your heart with passion?"

He scrawled out the information Pietr would need before tearing off the sheet from the legal pad and passing it to him. "Just find her. Please."

"Sûrement." His cousin took the paper, glancing at the cities, the dates, and the locations. "I pray God abandon any such plans of love for me. It is not a look which sits well on you."

Max grimaced. Pietr was right. He was obsessed. In love? Hardly. In lust? Absolutely. In trouble? That remains to be seen.

He'd returned to the ambassador's vault. The Fortunate Buddha hadn't been misplaced. It was definitely gone.

Did she go back for it? She had time while I met with the ambassador.

He glared out of the office window to the Paris sprawl beyond. The famed city of lovers, music, food, wine, and art. All he could think about were storm-gray eyes half-closed in pleasure.

The flat cam threw her off her game. She'd sought his help because of it. Max knew all of this. He couldn't have planned it better, but he'd not expected the reaction he would have when she'd looked so damn upset.

An expert thief, not even Interpol recorded much about her. She took from those who could not afford to report the losses. Even the livid ambassador would not report the absence of the Fortunate Buddha.

He'd preferred to threaten instead, accusing him of the theft. While he didn't give a damn what the ambassador thought of him personally, his impeccable reputation made him the go-to man for internal security systems. He worked for the best of the best, the elite. He could crack any security, and he tested all aspects of it.

Somehow, she'd managed to evade his security on three previous jobs. He'd been frustrated by the phantom until he'd worked out the connection to the beautiful vixen. Now she fascinated him. Max didn't care about the ambassador's motives or his questionable acquisition of the Buddha—why else wouldn't he report the loss?—but he wanted the truth.

If she didn't have the Buddha, a much greater problem existed for them in a common enemy.

Ferocity pulsed through him. Anya was out there, ignorant of the shadows' swirling plots threating to catch her unawares. Whoever had the disc knew what she looked like. Max's trap may have endangered her beyond anything she could imagine.

I have to get to her first.

He would.

**

"Good morning, James." Anya grinned as she arrived in her favorite shop. The couple behind the counters and their two sons had run the little eatery for decades. The little shop opened promptly at 6:00 a.m. and served a traditional fry-up, hot tea, and orange juice. The sturdy fare was her jam and crumpets whenever she returned to London.

The January morning had dawned cold and damp without a hint of sunshine on the horizon. The air carried the promise of snow. The idea of it made her wistful. She'd missed Christmas at home with the rousing rounds of snowball fights, snowmen, and hot cocoa in front of the fire while her parents argued over the merits of which Dickens story they should read aloud this year.

Snow in London just wasn't the same.

She'd dressed warmly, despite feeling quite at home in the chill—jeans, a rich chocolate-colored cashmere sweater, a white scarf, and a matching deep-brown trimmed white hat to keep her ears snug. The cable knit mukluks kept her feet warm.

"Good morning, missy. You'll be having the bacon today. The sausage is a bit tough, and you're too tender a Yank for it." James carried over the fresh pot of tea, orange juice, and the heavily laden plate with three fried eggs, potatoes, toast and jam, the aforementioned bacon, and a thick slice of ham. It was far too much food.

But they refused to give her anything less.

She plucked a piece of bacon off of her plate and chewed happily. *She shouldn't be obsessing about Maxwell Sauvage. He's the past. I live in the present. Time to move on.*

But those sexy bedroom eyes, skin shivering accent, and the way his words turned your insides to liquid.

Anya dropped her face into her hand and whistled a breath through her teeth. Her conscience, voice of reason, or inner monologue really needed a vacation.

Nope. Just need him.

If she started yelling at herself, they'd probably summon the men in the white coats. Instead, she concentrated on eating the bacon. When she finished it, she added jam to her toast and ate one of the eggs. Every action deliberate, every bite savored.

She'd been so focused on blocking out the little chit of a voice when she looked up and found the man in question staring at her, she dismissed it as a weak attempt at hallucination.

But the slow, devastating grin, the way the light hit his gorgeous face, and the purely masculine satisfaction glinting in his sexy bedroom eyes were either the best hallucinations ever, which meant she really needed to be medicated, or Max sat across the table from her.

In London.

In the little shop.

While she devoured a fry-up.

"Bonjour, pet. Miss me?"

Chapter Six

"**H**oly crap," were the first words that came to mind.

"I appreciate the sentiment, but I am not crap." He smiled again. The flash of those white teeth had a wild effect on her libido. He wore a dark-gray suit jacket over a plain gray sweater and relaxed trousers, every inch the image of an executive out for a comfortable breakfast before heading to the office, albeit a bit causally.

"What are you doing here?" How did you find me? Have I been compromised? Does Walter know? Oh, hell.

"Well, right now"—Max turned in the seat and lifted a finger to Michael—"I am ordering a cup of tea. Is the fry-up any good? The ham looks a little underdone."

"It's perfectly fine." She glared. He would not insult James or his wife or Michael with any criticism of their cooking. "Excellent, in fact."

She took up the knife and fork, cutting at the gristle around the edges of the ham slice just to prove it to him. Spearing a piece of the ham, she took a bite and smiled despite the fact it was a little undercooked and definitely too salty.

"Good to know."

The bastard laughed at her, but he said nothing as Michael brought a fresh pot and refilled both cups with steaming tea. She still grappled with the idea he sat here, in the little shop with its hard steel chairs, vinyl cushions, and plastic checkered table coverings.

Anya gave Michael a half-smile as he cleared away plates off the neighboring table. When he left, she leaned forward, hands on the edge of the table. "What are you doing here?" She enunciated each word as though it were followed by a period.

"I missed you." His simple, direct answer left her floundering. How had he found her? Had he tagged her?

Could he have learned the location of IAAR corporate from her?

Her mind whirled as she sorted and discarded the possibilities. She'd not slipped up. She'd left Rabat on a flight as Juliet Montague, a common enough code name with the requisite passport, credit cards, and backstopped identification. From Casablanca, she'd flown as Anya Lund. Nothing could connect the two names; she'd made sure of it.

So, how the hell had he tracked her down to her favorite little eatery in London? Where she was neither Anya Lund nor Juliet Montague?

"You know, a lesser man would be concerned by the way you're looking at me."

"Oh?" Her heart flopped around like a fish on the end of the line.

"I realize this might be a bit of a surprise for you, chérie—"

"Don't call me chérie."

"Pardon?"

"The endearment. Don't use it here." She slid a glance around the room. Nothing else had changed. James cooked. His wife Cynthia stood at the register, chatting up a friend, while Michael made quick work of cleaning the emptying tables.

The morning lull was her favorite time of day. Until now. Now it emphasized her isolation, alone, at the table with Maxwell Sauvage.

"And why not?"

"Because it's not appropriate here."

The corners of his mouth twitched. Damn the man. He laughed at her again. She stood, abruptly, pushing the chair away and fishing out several pound notes to leave on the table. It was too much, but she didn't care.

Somehow, he made it to the door before she did and held it open for her. The chill wind struck her as she stepped out, washing away the confusion and frustration his appearance riled up.

Crossing her arms across her chest and hunching her shoulders, she turned left, walking blindly. Thoughts of him had haunted her since she'd left Rabat. Excitement wrestled with worry over his appearance. She couldn't go to the flat.

Not with Max right here.

He fell into step next to her, his stride easily matching her clipped steps. The mukluks were a great idea when she'd gone for the dramatic look earlier in front of the mirror. Now she'd wished she'd just worn a pair of Nikes—so when she cut and run three streets up and used the interconnecting alleys behind the flats, she'd be able to ditch him.

Her mind worked to assess possibilities, escape routes, and the more gymnastics, the better. She'd learned her lesson very early in her career with the IAAR. She'd been the decoy for another agent, baiting a target to draw them away. The pursuit proved a near miss. She'd ended up with a dislocated shoulder after literally throwing herself off a building to get away from him.

A narrow escape, but she'd learned from it. She'd learned to keep her options open and to think ahead. Her shoulder ached at the memory. She didn't think Max could match him, and if he did, well, she had a Taser in her pocket for just such occasions.

Why am I thinking about Tasering him? Her first thought when she saw him again wasn't escape.

Far from it.

Time to get off the crazy train. She didn't know why he was there. She didn't know how he'd found her. Everything in her screamed caution. Use extreme caution.

Live and learn. Key the emphasis on the live.

"Where are we going, chérie? You look cold." He shucked out of his jacket. When he tried to drape it around her shoulders, she jerked away, throwing her arms out to keep him from closing the gap.

"Stop."

He froze, jacket in hand. His gaze held a mixture of curiosity and bafflement. "You're cold."

His expression of pure puzzlement tugged at her heart. She ignored the squeeze because the road to Hell was paved with these kinds of temptations.

"So?" Her brows raised in challenge. A wind chased errant leaves down the street and swirled between them.

He held up his hands in surrender and carefully put the jacket on. "Point taken."

"Why are you here?"

"I told you why."

"You missed me." She turned the phrase over, tasting a flavor too sweet to be believed. Could he be for real? Did she want it to be real?

"Yes." Irritation slid through the bafflement. A vein throbbed in

69

his forehead. Despite his play at relaxed demeanor, he was anything but.

For some strange reason, the hopping vein made her feel better. He wasn't as nonplussed by this encounter as he came across. Yes, he'd found her, and she still wanted to know how he'd done it—what was his agenda?

She needed to know, so she could adjust her actions accordingly.

Agendas were so much easier than missing.

He rolled his neck to the side; tension kept his shoulders stiff. It had taken him twenty-four hours and all of Pietr's resources to track her inside of London. He'd arrived first thing in the morning and headed out directly to meet with a contact when he'd seen her. At first, he'd been stupefied. She crossed out of a park, her sassy little hips bouncing as she trotted toward a corner shop advertising breakfast, coffee, and a selection of pastries.

He'd kept his distance, using his phone to capture her image when she'd sat down in the shop. The same image branded in his mind. Her full lips stretched into a wide, open grin. It wasn't the seductive invitation or the dangerous flirt, but a genuine smile. Her face was scrubbed free of any trace of makeup, and her luxurious hair hid under the stylish white hat.

But her eyes captivated him. In daylight, they looked darker, verging on storm clouds. It took ten minutes for Pietr to run the photograph against the airport composites they'd been able to buy. She was so utterly different from the vixen he'd met around the world and who'd shared his bed.

His body harbored no such illusions. He'd hardened the moment he saw her. When Pietr confirmed the images were facially matched, he'd told him to call off the search and shut it down. Then he'd watched her as she ordered her breakfast.

The little shop must have been a regular destination for her because she chatted up the staff with an open grin that made him ache to be the recipient of it. When the waiter flirted, he swallowed the urge to pound him in the face.

He'd planned to wait for her to finish and then follow her home. He needed time to formulate his approach, to smooth the choppy waters ahead. But when her face softened and her teeth dug into her lower lip, he groaned. His body wanted her, right here and right now, and his mind wasn't disagreeing.

Walking into the shop and sitting across from her took every ounce of his considerable control. Now, standing in the middle of the street, earning more than a few curious looks from Londoners heading about, anger stirred. He didn't want to see her cold, and she acted like he'd assaulted her.

"You're cold," he repeated. "But, if you prefer the chill, then by all means." He motioned for her to proceed, but she continued to glare at him.

What was it about this slender, athletic woman? She'd looked spectacular at the New Year's ball in her barely there dress, and she'd looked even better when she lay beneath him on the bed. Yet, standing on the damp and windy street with fire crackling around every word, she took his breath away.

"Tell me why you are here, Max. Here in London. Here at my shop. Don't give me some song and dance about missing me. We barely know each other."

"Don't we?" A splinter of hurt stabbed through his pleasure at seeing her. She really didn't want him here. But does she not want me here in London or in her life?

Too bad, on either account.

She closed her eyes, and he frowned. He didn't want her to look away from him. He enjoyed watching the emotions collide in those cool depths. How he could have ever believed she measured control escaped him. He liked the raw fire he saw there.

Tired of the odd looks, he took her elbow in hand and gently nudged her toward the park he could see across the street. She jerked her elbow away and glared at him.

"Anya, can we talk?"

"If you can promise to not manhandle me."

His turn to count to ten. He grimaced, holding his temper in check. It was usually easier than this, but something about her turned his brain to mush and his body to one of a randy youngster at his first Eton formal.

"I will endeavor to keep my hands to myself—at least until you ask for them again." He smiled. She would want his hands on her. She'd wanted them in Rabat. She'd want them here.

When she swallowed, he nearly regretted the issue of the promise. But he'd made it. He would stick to it. He was a man of his word. Or at least he'd always been. If she flicked her pink tongue over her lips again, he would be putting those words to the test.

"All right." She breathed in agreement and nodded toward the park. He considered offering his arm but thought better of it and motioned for her to take the lead.

He didn't mind following. He'd never been overly fond of denim on women, but the way the jeans hugged her pert little bottom caused his own pants to constrict painfully. He grunted a sound and shook his head when she looked at him in inquiry.

On any normal, warm day, the park would be laden with children and families walking their dogs, picnicking on blankets, running, and generally enjoying the park's environs. Overcast skies and chilly breezes emptied the park of all but the hardiest of souls.

And Anya.

He said nothing, judging the brisk walk as a way to take the edge off her temper. On the side road, just beyond the park wall, a black sedan slipped into a residential space. Three men wearing black-on-black business suits emptied out of the vehicle and began paralleling their course.

Her brow wrinkled into a frown. "So, just spit it out whatever it is so we can get back to our lives."

Not good.

He cupped a hand under her elbow, fingers tightening when she went to jerk away. He dropped his head in a casual manner. "Need to walk faster, luv."

"What?" Her cold glare scorched him.

He enjoyed the hell out of her fiery temperament, but they didn't have time to waste sparring. One of the three slipped through a wall gate and ambled nearer. The men might be about their own business, but a surreptitious glance told him the black sedan wasn't idling at the curb but angling ahead, toward the opposite end of the park.

A second man joined the first, cutting across the park behind them.

Boxing them in.

She stopped abruptly and jerked her arm away. "I get it. You've got a thing for me. Great, but, clearly, I'm not interested at the moment. So save the he-man tactics, yeah?"

Breath hissing between his teeth, Max closed the distance between them, hands cupping her face. Her pupils dilated, and he caught her sudden inhale. A fierce possessiveness flamed through him. She wasn't as disinterested as she pretended. Too bad he couldn't take the time to show her just how disinterested she wasn't.

"We've got company, luv. So let's schedule this argument for later."

Her attention skated past his shoulder. Stiffness evaporated from her posture, and her stormy eyes darkened with predatory thunderclouds. "You brought company with you?" The mild accusation carried enough disbelief to make him smile.

"Not intentionally, I promise." He slid an arm around her and nudged her to resume walking. Their audience followed less than ten yards away.

"Maybe you should walk away." She'd torn a page from his book, her words a tense whisper.

Max glared, offended at the suggestion. If these were the ambassador's men, he wasn't abandoning her to their less than tender mercies. He wasn't abandoning her, period.

"You have an opportunity here...." She slipped a few inches between them but didn't shrug off his arm. Her steps grew more purposeful.

"Don't." He studied the area. The farther they cut across the park, the more isolated it became. They couldn't angle toward the wall without cutting across their audience's path. Ahead, the black sedan prowled, a sleek and silent sentry, watching.

"Max?" A curious, taut note in her voice yanked his attention toward the man heading toward them on their left.

Five men.

He'd seen three get out of the car.

One driver.

The fifth must have entered the park just behind them, shadowing their wake.

"I'm serious. Maybe you should get out of here."

He growled. "Get ready to run."

"Max!"

He ignored her shout, skirting around her and catching the man on their left with a hard cut to the cheek, striking with the edge of his hand. The blow staggered the man, hopefully blurring his vision and leaving him out of it for the next few seconds. Pounding feet rushed toward his right, but Max turned, weight rolling onto the balls of his feet as he stiff-armed a second man in the throat. He gagged and went down choking.

A third caught Anya around her middle and jerked the slender woman off her feet. Max hurtled toward them when she peeled the man's thumb back, a sharp crack breaking the breathy silence. She met his eyes for one wild instant before she slammed her head backward, catching her assailant in the face. Blood spouted from his nose, and he released her with a howl.

One swipe from his meaty hand caught her in the shoulder and sent her spinning. A tackle took Max down to the hard-packed earth, sending sparks of pain through his knee. He rolled with the tackle, yanking the attacker over and slamming him into the ground.

Wind rushed past his head, Anya struck the second man who came at them, with a roundhouse to the solar plexus. His agile little nymph didn't slow as she spun around, shifting her weight and snapping a second kick into the man's face.

Max rose and then dropped, elbow connecting with his attacker's groin. He cut off the man's high-pitched yelp as he grabbed his head and slammed him to the ground. Scrambling to his feet, he saw the fourth man running toward them, a pistol in his hand.

Seizing Anya's hand, he kicked the man with the broken nose as he fought to get to his feet and ran. They didn't have a gun. The bark of the pistol kicked up dirt to his left. Dragging her with him, he headed for the wall and brace of townhouses along the side street. She raced next to him, shooting frantic glances behind her without breaking pace.

"Two of them are up."

"Run now, talk later." His knee protested their speed, but he ignored it. At the wall, he turned to give her a leg up, but she went up and over without any assistance from him. Laughter wheezed out, and he grabbed the brick lip and hauled himself after her.

A second shot hit the brick next to his head, shrapnel burning his ear. One street over, police sirens punched through the air.

"Must go faster." She tugged him to his feet, taking the lead. Her hand grasping his, she dashed between park cars and raced across the street. The black sedan barreled toward them, but they ignored it.

A paved sidewalk led between the cottage flats and twisted behind the bricked private gardens. She turned a sharp right, rushing thirty yards and then jerking him left. He shot a glance over his shoulder, not trusting they could outrun the pursuers. Every instinct in his body screamed to take them out so they couldn't pursue, but his heart and head overruled those baser instincts.

The men were armed.

Anya could get hurt.

"Here!" she barked, hardly slowing as she dropped his hand and slithered up a brick wall. Her fingers and toes found minute handholds. She straddled the top and reached a hand down to him. Pride smarting, he ignored the offer and jumped, grabbing the lip and hauled himself up.

She snorted and dropped to the soft grass on the other side. He followed suit, his knee snapping in protest.

"Straight across and over the other wall. King Street on the other side. Cut across. Yellow house on the corner; there's a tuck wall hiding their side street. It's old cobbles. Too narrow for their car." She didn't wait for him to acknowledge her instructions, sprinting around the garden's pond and over the wall. Admiration torched as he lunged after her. She moved like Jet Li, hardly slowing as fingers and toes found invisible grasping points.

He followed her, relying on brute strength and speed to keep up with her finesse. Across the road and down the cobblestone path, she switched direction four more times, always behind buildings and out of sight of the street, not slowing for several minutes.

Lungs burning, he let out a whoosh of relief as they darted down stone steps toward the tube. She slowed to a leisurely walk and threaded her arm through his.

Two people.

Out for a mid-morning stroll.

Tourists.

Londoners.

It didn't matter.

Anya produced a card for the turnstile and passed it to him after she went through. He followed, working on slowing his harsh breathing.

"So." She grinned as the tube arrived and the doors slid open on cue. The announcer's staid "Mind the gap," echoed over her words. "You were saying...."

Laughter, drunk with adrenaline, rolled out of him. He dropped onto a seat next to her, watching the doors cautiously until they closed and the tube whisked them away toward Notting Hill Station.

"You left without saying good-bye." Not where he intended to start.

"You knew I was going. You knew before you arrived in my hotel room. You knew before you joined me in the shower...." She twisted sideways in the seat and cupped her hand to the side of his head. The sting of a cloth pressing on his ear reminded him of the shrapnel.

"And the counter, the floor, and the bed. I remember, chérie. I remember very well. But you didn't even leave a note." He skimmed his eyes over her. Her wrinkled clothes, smudged with dirt, betrayed their mad dash.

"Look. I appreciated your help. But you got what you wanted. You got me in bed, and I don't see why you're acting like I ran off with the family silver when you looked away." She kept up the pressure on his ear.

"So that is why you slept with me, then? Because I assisted you?" He would not beg her. He gripped the back of the chairs in front of them, squeezing his fist in a modicum of control over his temper.

"No. I told you I wouldn't trade for your help, but you asked."

"Then why did you have sex with me, chérie? Why did you make love to me with fervent passion? Why did you reach for me time and time again?" He pitched the words low, aware of the other passengers huddled in their detached worlds, riding toward their destinations.

Pink suffused her cheeks, and if he didn't know any better, he would say she blushed. She turned her face away, a startled bird. The train rocked to a stop in Notting Hill Station. Her hand fell away from his ear, the handkerchief vanishing into her jean pocket before she tucked the collar of his shirt into his jacket. He shoved fingers through his hair to hide the injury. They stood together, weaving through the exiting passengers and flowing up the stairs.

"I slept with you because I wanted to." She said it softly. "You're a good-looking guy. You helped me out. You can be a lot of fun. But that's all it was. A good time."

"Your mouth says one thing, but your eyes say something else. And if I was such a good time, why then would you be upset at the idea of seeing me again, chérie? I assure you, I would have no problems in showing you a good time again."

Anya scowled. "You're such an arrogant bastard."

"I assure you, my paternity has never been in question."

She rolled her eyes, but her lips quirked. Then she began laughing. The magical sound drained his anger away.

"I notice you aren't disputing the charge of arrogance."

"Why should I?" He lifted his shoulders. Thick traffic flowed through the street in front of them. "Arrogance is the belief in one's best qualities. I assure you, I believe in them and I have confidence you do as well."

She laughed again, a warm chuckle rolling up from her belly like a geyser. He loved the sound of it. She'd made those sounds when he tickled her during lovemaking. Her inner thighs were particularly sensitive. If he nibbled there, her body thrashed, and her moans turned to laughter.

"What are you thinking about?" she asked, amusement still ringing in her voice.

"You, chérie."

"Really? You were looking a little strained around the edges."

"I was remembering how you felt when I ran my fingers over your stomach. How sweet you tasted. How you writhed when I kissed your belly, your thighs and...." He didn't care who heard them now.

"Woah!" She stepped into him and put her cold fingers against his lips. The touch sizzled through him. This near, she smelled of lilacs and vanilla. He remembered the sweet flavor of cherries in her kiss. Her lips were parted, her tongue just peeking past her teeth as she gazed at him. He kissed the tips of her fingers, half-expecting her to snatch them away.

"You asked me what I was thinking," he murmured between kisses.

Her pupils dilated, and he could hear the catch in her throat as she tried to breathe. "I didn't." She swallowed. "I mean, I didn't realize what you were thinking about."

"It's all I have been able to think about." He kissed her ring finger then her middle then her index once more. Her hand hovered there, touching him, electricity pulsing from her cool fingers to his heated flesh.

"Max, us getting involved is not a good idea."

"Why not?" He took a chance and narrowed the space between them, but she didn't retreat. Her fingers slid along his cheek, and he wanted to purr in satisfaction at the gentle caress.

"It...it's just not."

"Very succinct, but hardly...." He bent his head, inhaling the sweet scent of her shampoo. Citrus. Like the hotel room. Lilacs and vanilla perfumed her skin, but he smelled California's orange groves in her hair.

She inhaled as he inched closer until their faces nearly touched, but he kept his hands still, aware of his promise. The city faded away around them.

"You want me, Anya. I know you do." He ached to take her in

his arms but had promised he wouldn't lay a finger on her again, not until she asked him to. Who knew a promise could kill? "God knows, I want you."

To his delight, her startled groan slipped out. Her fingers stroked up his cheek to twist in his hair. He acquiesced to her tug, which brought his mouth into contact with hers.

Sweet, pliant lips opened to his invasion. No, begged for it. Her tongue dueled with his, tasting and tempting him. Her teeth grazed lightly, and she rose up on her tiptoes, pressing her slender form to him. He could feel the weight of her breasts through the sweater and the soft steel of her legs seeking him.

"Luv...." he whispered into the kiss. Keeping his hands away from her was pure torture. But he tasted her, he savored the flavor of her lips, and he demanded more. She broke away, but hunger lit her eyes.

"You really do want me."

"I did not lie about my eagerness for you, luv. Never that."

She panted, hands still clutching him. "This can never work."

"We do not even know what this is. How can you know whether it will work or not?"

"Because...." She pushed away, and he jammed his hands into his pockets to keep from catching her. She worried at her lips, her swollen lips. Pure masculine triumph shot through him. She enjoyed his kisses.

"I am waiting, chérie. Tell me."

"You're impossible."

"I disagree. I am completely possible. Were we not in public, you could be exploring the possibility right now." Tipping his head to the right, he gave her a gentle nudge. "And speaking of being in public, we should go and get off the streets. I have a car, but it's compromised, and we can walk to my hotel from here."

"Hotel?" She frowned. "Don't you have a house here?"

"Oui. But it's two hours away, and I find if we want to delve into these possibilities you are worried about and sample them, then I would like to get to it right away."

She shivered, and he knew this time it wasn't from the cold. He wanted her to come with him. He wanted her out of the line of fire. He wanted to lay her down and make love to her. He wanted to stand her up and make love to her. He wanted her under him and over him. Tension coiled within him, eager for release.

If he could assuage his need for her, they could focus on their problems. He needed to convince her to come with him. He suspected she would reject him going to her home, and he would accept her rejection.

For now.

"I see your point." She seemed to struggle for control. The husky quality of her voice pulled at him. "This is a mistake."

"Talking like this?" Her mind seemed to fly from one extreme to the other; he found it difficult to keep up.

"Going with you."

"It will not be a mistake, chérie." He smiled. She was going with him.

"No, it's a mistake." But she wasn't walking away.

"Then why come with me?"

"It could be we just survived an armed assault in the park."

"It could be." He nodded gamely.

"It could be your determination to see me again."

"Definitely."

"And it could be I missed you, too."

He grinned, and, this time, he offered his arm.

When their bodies met, lightning sizzled through her system, burning away all the awkwardness of their reunion. He shouldn't be there in London, but he was. He shouldn't have been able to track her down, but he had. She shouldn't be naked in his arms, kissing the hell out of him, but she was.

They'd retreated to his hotel room, and, all the way up the lift, she lectured herself on the reasons this was a bad idea. She did not scope out his ass as he stepped out on the upper floor. Nor did she give him points for bracing the lift entrance until she could exit. Her gaze did not linger on his lips, nor did she think about how wonderfully thick his cock was or how damn talented with it he was.

No, she didn't. She formed a reasonable, rational response to their situation and prepared to brainstorm a solution. A solution which involved him leaving and her disappearing—only it ended when he blotted out all objections as his tongue stroked sensuously along hers.

His fingers ran lightly over her skin, drawing her to the intoxicating precipice she'd merrily jumped off in Morocco. She tried to block out the luxury suite, the decorative ceiling, and she just let herself feel as his lips stroked down her throat and then latched onto the turgid point of one nipple. Blood surged through her.

His hands seemed to be everywhere, stripping her clothing off, cupping a breast, teasing a nipple. His fingers danced down over the swell of her ass, lifting her off the ground until her legs scissored around his hips. His cock nestled against her slick entrance, gliding along the cotton fabric of her panties separating them.

His breath rasped as he walked them deeper into the suite. Her nails sank into his shoulders. They should have paused to take care of the cut on his ear, but if it didn't bother him.... She let the thought trail away. Frustration and anticipation twined together, soaking her panties with need. A low moan speared through her, and she wasn't sure who made the sound.

Pressure pushed down through her belly, a great weight coalescing in her sex. She cried out when he dropped her on the bed. The panties ripped down her legs, cold air rushing in to kiss her slick skin. She barely recognized herself in the throes of this mad passion, but she had to touch him. Her fingers glided over the smooth, muscled planes of his chest and down to the thick weight of his cock jutting toward her in demand.

Licking her lips, she leaned in to kiss the crown. Max hissed and jerked away. "Non, I will not last." Foil tore and she watched, in a daze, as he rolled the condom into place. His body jerked toward her, and his hands scooped under her ass, lifting her hips up as her shoulders dug into the bed.

"I wanted to take my time, but soon...first...." His words were harsh, labored and, somewhere in the haze of passion sheening her vision, she realized he was as desperate for this as she was. She arched her hips, spreading her legs obediently, aching to meet his demand with her own. His sheathed cock bumped her clit, slipping over the moisture beading along the labia, nudging her entrance, and, as if his patience snapped, he thrust inside of her.

His body pushed into hers, pushing, stretching, and filling her tightly. Her moan ripped out of her throat, and she watched as he lifted her hips and the slow stretch ended as he began to rock his hips. He controlled every thrust. His fingers dug into her hips, not allowing her any respite, and she was torn between flying apart at the sensations blowing through her and wanting him to drive harder.

His muscles rippled with controlled force, surging into her and blotting out coherent thought. His rhythm dominated her, demanded her focus, her adoration, her worship, and, when carnal tension knotted in her belly, she screamed for release.

"Say it." He pushed the words through a grimace. "Say my name."

Her body trembled on the edge of the orgasm he tormented her with, her sex gripping and releasing him in alternating rhythm to his thrusts. She arched her back, but she had no leverage. Her pleasure lay in his hands—and, damn him, he knew it. She surrendered.

"Please, Max...."

The words seemed to detonate within him as his hips picked up their tempo and he adjusted his grip to stroke one thumb across her swollen clit, undoing her completely.

Max....

Anya sprawled across the bed, lazily tracing finger patterns over his chest. "I don't want to move."

"Then don't." An answer for everything. *He was dangerous, had been from their first encounter in the lounge of the Moscow airport, and damn easy to talk to.*

Easy to provoke.

Too easy to want more with.

She'd known in Florence, in Prague, and in Paris. She'd known it from the moment she saw him in Rabat—the day before she made her play for the Fortunate Buddha. She saw him, and she wanted him. Dipping her head, she traced the path of her finger with her tongue. He tasted of salt and man.

"What are you thinking about now, chérie?" He watched her with those lazy, brooding eyes which could flame with so much passion. *Perhaps he'd finally spent himself, and she found herself wondering if she could rouse his passion again.*

"Honestly, I wonder if the bathroom is as hedonistic as the rest of this place." *And who those men were. But talking about it now brings us to reality. I am rather enjoying this sojourn in fantasy.*

"I should hope so. I stay here often, and I enjoy a little hedonism." He grinned. "We could go and test the facilities if you like."

"Hmm...." She considered the idea. "That would require moving, and I don't think I have any bones left." *They weren't IAAR. Walter wouldn't send a goon squad to collect me. They followed Max.*

"Ahh, then it is a good thing we can summon room service. I will be able to still feed you even if you can't leave the bed."

His skin was warm and dark, more Greek in his tan than she would have expected. She ran her fingers down his side and marveled at the rippling muscles across his abdomen.

As promised, she found a hedonistic paradise with twin showerheads and water pressure to die for in the bathroom. She washed away the sweat of their pleasure. She loved London, but London in winter could be a chilly place. The heavenly shower helped ease her aches.

Wrapped in a thick, terry cloth towel, she padded into the bedroom and frowned. Her clothes were gone. She followed the sound of voices into the living room and flashed a smile at the porter delivering their room service. Max scowled at her standing in the open doorway, all bare legs and arms with only a towel to protect her modesty.

"One moment, chérie." He turned to the porter and pressed the check wallet to his chest and shoved him toward the door. "That will be all, thank you."

The boy stammered and vanished. Max shut the door with a thump and gave her another reproving look.

"What?"

"You should not parade about half-nude in front of strangers."

"Well, I would have gotten dressed, but my clothes seem to have taken a walk, and I didn't see any of yours in the closet, which means you aren't really staying here and likely just booked the room. And, speaking of which, should we really be staying somewhere under your name if they are after you?"

"It is of no importance." He smiled, inserting the screw into the cork and working it free so the wine could breathe. "The hotel is far too public."

"One could make the same argument about a public park in London with CCTV cameras everywhere, but I didn't notice it slowing them down."

"A calculated gamble, one they failed. Would you press the point by going more public in a secure hotel?"

"No. Unless I had a way around the security." She could concede the point. After all, a man with Max's money could pretty much do whatever he wanted. He could probably buy a new wardrobe no matter what city he stayed in. "Fine. So we're safe for now. Where are my clothes?"

"I will get you a robe if you like. I sent your things to be cleaned."

"They weren't so dirty."

"True, chérie. But I did not wish to find you dressed and out the door as quickly this time. I've ordered a meal—several dishes, in fact—because I wasn't sure what you would care for. I can go and take a shower now, if you will promise me you will be here when I come out."

"And if I'm not here?" She lifted her chin. She wasn't a trophy or a prize to be locked up. She wouldn't stand for it. She'd strut out of the hotel in the towel if necessary.

Though his manner seemed even and measuring, beneath his calm veneer, she knew his passion stirred in volcanic proportions. "Then I would find you again."

It was an oath.

She nodded slowly. The fierceness in his vow and his eyes should warn her away, but she wasn't afraid of it. If she were to be completely honest, she found herself liking his possessiveness. Had she completely lost her mind?

After dropping the damp towel, she strolled over to him, unabashed and pleased by the desire crossing his face. "Then I'll be right here waiting for you." She sat on the sofa and crossed one leg over the other. *And your answers.* Despite herself, she was curious about the park assault. *Who are they, and what the hell do they want?*

He groaned and shook his head. "You are a vixen."

"I've been called worse."

"Only by fools. I will hurry. Eat if you are hungry. I have a great deal I would like to talk to you about." He caressed her cheek before striding off to the bathroom, purposefulness to his step as though he wanted to complete the task as quickly as possible and return to her.

She chuckled then stared at the ceiling. She could smell salmon, vegetables, and there was a teapot with the wine. A few bottles of soda were even stashed under the wheeled cart.

Stomach grumbling, she rolled off the sofa and stalked over to explore what he'd ordered. Cucumber sandwiches, grilled salmon, steaming rice, fried vegetables, even a plate of fish and chips, and one large steak, medium rare. Her stomach rumbled at the assault on her senses. She stole one of the chips and nibbled on it.

"I thought you might like something on there."

She jumped. He stood in the bedroom door, staring at her in a ravenous manner. He wore a towel slung around his hips, and his hair was still dripping from the shower. He'd wasted no time.

"I think I like everything here."

"Everything?" He crossed toward, captured her face in his hands, and bent down to kiss her, slowly, lovingly.

Lovingly.

Anya twisted away from him and stole another chip to give herself something to do besides kiss him. Her pulse raced at high speed, leaving her breathless and struggling.

"Chérie?"

"It's all good." She gave him a quick flash of a smile. "I'm just hungry."

"Then eat, and here"—he tossed her a robe she hadn't seen in his hands—"put this on."

"You don't like me in this?" She motioned to her nude body and thankfully fresh-shaven legs.

"I love you like that, but you won't be eating much food if you do not cover it up for me to unwrap later."

Shivers chased up her spine at the word later. Is he suggesting a relationship? We're hell and gone past one-night stand.

She slid the terry cloth robe on. He took control of the cart and wheeled it over to the table for two by the windows. Outside, London sprawled, redolent with the capriciousness of both age and whimsy.

Anya strolled over and slid into the seat opposite him, tucking one leg beneath her.

"Do you have a preference?"

"Hmm, I'll take a truthful explanation and some salmon, please."

"Interesting palate for one who seems allergic to the truth. I will take the steak if you have no objections."

"Only if the truth bites."

"But of course." He filled their plates. The hair at the nape of his neck curled ever so slightly as it dried. He caught her watching and smiled.

So very domestic.

Another shiver chased up her spine. At her shudder, he frowned. "I will turn up thermostat. You're cold."

She didn't correct his assumption and simply smiled in gratitude.

"Would you prefer wine or tea?"

"Water will be fine. Who were those men?" His presence was intoxicating enough. She needed to stop being so muddle-headed about everything.

"Still?" He picked up a bottle of chilled water and cracked the seal on it before pouring it into a glass. He chose wine for himself.

"I'm not going to have an affair with you," she blurted then chased her humiliating declaration with a swallow of the cold water.

Max sat down and unrolled his napkin, his expression equally amused and curious. "Bon. But I do not recall asking you to have an affair."

Of course he hadn't asked. Idiot. She took another sip and then set her glass aside. "But isn't that what this chasing me is all about?"

"Sadly." He speared a piece of the blood-red meat with his fork and sighed. "No, chérie, that is not what this is all about."

A chill curled around her stomach, freezing the food she'd already eaten into an uncomfortable lump. "Then what is it about?"

She could barely stand to chew the delicious salmon. The tart mixture of lemon and spices tasted like dead wood. She worked her jaw slowly and swallowed the bite with the help of another sip of water.

Dread was not a friendly dinner companion.

He reached across the table to take her hand. "Let us eat first, have the pretense of a good meal, and then we will talk of more serious matters, please."

Anya shivered again, only this time it wasn't the cold.

Chapter Seven

He watched her push the food around on the plate. Despite their escapade in the park, he'd enjoyed the morning and would have prolonged it save for the call from Pietr while she showered.

The ambassador had hired men to locate his Buddha. They were targeting anyone close to Max. Pietr could handle himself, but the guards remembered her from the ambassador's house. They remembered their interlude in the bedroom.

They were looking for Anya.

They'd found her, too.

Did I bring them right to her? Pietr wanted him on the plane out of England. A private security detail watched over his jet.

"You're Interpol, aren't you?" she demanded. The question, so unexpected, actually earned a laugh from him and another glare from her.

He held up his hands, surrendering. "No, Anya. I am not."

"You could be lying."

"Perhaps. But law enforcement is not something I am involved in. Of course, were I Interpol, I would have arrested you the moment you revealed you took the Fortunate Buddha, which I did not." He needed to be patient and rational. He needed to lay out the argument in clear, concise measures, so she would not react badly.

"All right." The stiffness in her shoulders relaxed, but she remained wary, watching him for some sign of a ruse. He could appreciate her position.

"I am not with law enforcement. I have a job I do from time to time for certain clients who can afford my services."

She gave up any pretense of eating, cradling her glass of water in both hands, listening.

He tossed his napkin next to the plate and pinched the bridge of his nose. This confession would cost him. He could not pretend otherwise.

"What do you do for your clients?"

His silence must have worn on her, for she asked the question he needed to answer.

"I provide a form of security. I test their security, I crack it, and I show them where it is weak."

"And then you fix it for them?" The sun tried to peer through the cloud cover beyond the window, casting her in an ethereal light. Her auburn hair gleamed, and her stormy-gray eyes beckoned him for understanding.

"No, I never fix their security. Repairing it wouldn't be fun for me. It is only my job to show them their weaknesses. They can fix them or not as they see fit."

"I wouldn't expect someone with royal blood to need a job."

"Need one? No. Desire one. Yes. You see, I enjoy pitting my mind against theirs. I like to crack their security systems. I like to find a way past the greatest of encryptions, a flaw, perhaps, but it is what I like to do."

"So it's a hobby?" She relaxed again. He let out a breath. He wanted her to relax. He didn't want her to bolt from the room or to see mistrust and fury taint their connection.

"For lack of a better term, yes. A hobby which comes with a very exclusive client list."

"I guess it would have to. You can hardly advertise in the Royal Times." She took the revelation so much better than he'd thought possible.

"No. My clients are word of mouth. Private endorsements. Suggestions. I decide whether or not I will take a job and what fee I will charge."

"Okay. Doesn't sound so bad. You call the shots and you make the hours. I can see why it would be appealing. So, the men in the park were disgruntled clients?"

"After a fashion. A moment longer, Anya, please." At her nod, Max looked at the wine in the glass and swirled it. The truth tasted far more unpleasant than he'd imagined. "That part of the job is very lucrative and appealing to me. But there are drawbacks."

"Such as?" Despite her façade of relaxation, she didn't eat. She studied him, perhaps waiting for the other Blahnik to drop. Sadly, he would not be disappointing her on the matter.

"Such as adding my own surprises to their security system out of sheer curiosity about a certain thief who evaded better systems in the past."

Her shoulders went rigid, and her chin came up. "The flat cam."

"Oui."

"You set me up."

He wanted to say no. "Oui."

She stared. "Wow. I had no idea you wanted to bed me so badly."

"Non," he growled and slammed his hand down onto the table, making the china and silverware jump. "I did not place the flat cam there to compromise you. I put it there because I was curious. In Florence, you snatched the painting from a system I'd secured. You did it again with a manuscript in Paris. When the ambassador contacted me about the addition to his collection, I suspected it might be a lure to you. I wanted...."

"You wanted what? To make a fool out of me? To watch me twist in the wind?"

"No, I wanted to see how you did it. I admire skill. You are tremendously skilled. You are a puzzle. An enigma. I wanted...."

"You wanted to crack my code. Fantastic." She shoved her chair back and lunged away from him.

He went after her, refusing to let her leave until he told her the whole ugly truth of it. "Wait."

She fought him, and he blocked, locking his arms around her and hauling her to his chest. He could love this tiny and fierce woman so easily.

She rammed her knee toward his privates, and he barely shifted her in time to avoid blinding agony. Her next blow caught him in the crook of the elbow, and his hand went numb, releasing her.

"I told you to stop manhandling me." Gone was the waif with her softness promising hours of pleasure. In her place stood the spitting hellcat who took down two men in the park, and her expression promised fierce retribution.

"You're not going anywhere." He gritted the words out. Furious at her anger. Furious at his culpability in the situation. Furious with whomever took the damn tapes holding the strings to them both. "There is more, and I need you to hear it."

"More? Seriously? You set me up. You screwed me over, and then you screwed me...a lot." Anger colored the last words. Pain flickered through her eyes before she shuttered them.

Max held up his hands and retreated a step, choking off the insult burning in his gut and giving her room to calm down. "I did not set out to create a trap to force you to put the Buddha back. It shocked me when you came to me in the ballroom. Yes, I may have taken some advantage of the situation, but I helped you return it at your request. I helped you without the promise of your body."

"Well, aren't you the fortunate one. You still got it."

"Yes." He fought the urge to grab her again and sucked in a deep, patient breath. "I am the fortunate one. I was and am very grateful to have you, and I am grateful again for the hotel, and I am grateful right now. None of my gratitude has anything to do with the Buddha, the flat cam, or the theft."

"What theft? I put it back."

"That's just it, mon petite. Someone else took the Fortunate Buddha after we returned him. And they took the flat cam and the captured images of you. The Buddha is gone, and the evidence you were involved is out of my hands."

"And the men in the park?"

"The ambassador wants his property. He's convinced we have it."

Anya was going to throw up.

She stared at him. He wasn't lying. He gripped his arm where she'd struck with her elbow. His chest rose and fell rapidly, indicating his shallow breaths. The corners of his eyes pinched tight on the anger shining in them. Anger and something else. Something resembling a plea or an apology, but she jerked her hand down, slicing the thought in half.

It didn't matter. He'd set her up.

Dammit, he'd set her up.

When he made a move toward her again, she grabbed a lamp off the closest table and wielded it like a weapon. She wasn't above fighting dirty. She knew how to use everything in her environment. She would kick, scratch, bite, and throw everything she possessed if it came down to it.

He held up his hand to ward her off, pointedly limping to sit at the table. She wasn't fooled by his placid behavior. Quiet passion simmered under his cool exterior, bubbling just beneath the surface. So what has him so upset? The missing Buddha? The attempt on his life? Her role in the theft?

He planted the damn flat cam. Bile burned in her throat. He'd set her up.

Set.

Her.

Up.

She'd fucked him. Hell, she'd done a whole lot more than just fuck him. She played with him, adored on him, and even been happy to see him. She compromised her ethical standards, threatened her standing with the IAAR, and gambled her future. Her mind reeled with the possibilities.

Face it, toots, good guy or manipulative bastard, you fucked him because you wanted to and you still want him—manipulations and all.

"Let's clarify this, shall we? Hypothetically, I entered the vault through some nefarious means. I took the Fortunate Buddha from the stand and escaped the way I came in. Only, on my way out, I found an undocumented camera located well above the floor which caught my every action. I then sought a way to return the Buddha by approaching another thief."

Surprise wandered across his expression. "You think I'm a thief?"

"I knew you were something. You kept showing up at too many jobs. I saw you in Paris. I saw you get through a security system like it wasn't there. Of course, now I know you had the plans, so of course you did."

"I didn't need their plans." She'd stung his pride.

Good.

"Whatever. You were somewhere you shouldn't have been. You're ridiculously rich. Who would notice if you bent, broke, or maimed a few laws along your way."

"I would."

"Again, whatever. The point is I thought you were a thief. I knew you were interested in me, so I went to you for help."

An unhappy smile curled his lips. "Ahh, so you used the promise of your body to seduce my aid."

"I planned to use it to get you to do what I wanted and then leave without paying up."

His bark of laughter made her jump. "I do not know whether to applaud your temerity or strangle you right now."

"Join the club."

"Oh, I do not believe we are a club. You are offended I used deception to learn more about you and managed to seduce you when it's exactly what you planned to do—only your plan promised no satisfaction."

"I think you've been plenty satisfied."

"As have you, chérie."

"Stop calling me that!" The endearment irritated her. The inflection in his voice, the softening in his expression all created a fluttering in her stomach. She didn't want the tingles or the fluttering.

"No. I like calling you chérie."

Bastard. He wanted to be under her skin. Fine. He could be under it. Time to go.

"I think you can keep my clothes." She tightened the belt on the robe. "I can take a taxi downstairs."

"Anya, if you run, I will follow you, and I will find you."

"Hmm, that sounds suspiciously like a threat."

"No, it's a promise. You are in danger because of me. I will not leave you unprotected."

"Danger? Because someone else pinched the Buddha?" She shrugged. "It's a big world and a big playing field. Besides, how do I even know you don't have both tucked away. You were the last one in the vault. You were the last one in possession of the Buddha."

"The ambassador doesn't care. He cares you were there. He cares we spent time together." The frustration in his barked tone mimicked the frustration banding her chest.

"So, I'm a target because you're a target."

"No, you're a target because the Fortunate Buddha is gone."

"I didn't steal it!"

"Didn't you?"

She glared. "I put it back."

"No, you gave it to me, and I put it back."

"And I only have your word."

"Oui. You wanted to steal it, and, in fact, you did. You could have seen the codes I entered, retraced our steps after leaving the hotel room, and retrieved the Buddha after implicating me in its return."

"But I didn't."

"And I only have your word."

Logical. If he was guilty of the theft, why bother finding her at all? Why give her this whole song and dance? Why not just throw her to the ambassador's men? It didn't make sense. But she hadn't returned. She'd abandoned the profile by returning the idol then scrubbed the mission and extracted, following the parameters in place for leaving.

"So, you hunted me down to warn me?"

"You believe me about the Buddha, then?"

"I didn't say I did."

"Non," he conceded. "You did not. And that is fair enough. But you are not so angry now. I see you're beginning to think it through. You are a fascinating creature and a little bit frightening when you are so mad."

"You would do well to remember it."

"I will hardly forget." His tone dry, he gestured with a show of the gallant to the chair opposite him. "Will you stay, please?"

"Why?"

"Because through my actions, harm may come to you, and I will not allow it to happen."

"I am more than capable of taking care of myself."

"True. You were remarkable in the park. But they've seen what you can do now, and they have guns. You rely on your anonymity. You do not have such protection now if the one who took the Buddha also has the image of you on the flat cam."

"Why would they care? I mean, woo hoo, they have a video of me. They also have stolen property. To get one, they would have to get the other." Still, she returned to the chair and sat. Exhaustion wound through her as her anger leaked away. His plausible story and honorable intentions were compelling.

Bastard.

Agreed.

"I do not know why they would care. I do know the ambassador is livid you violated security. With the Buddha taken, he is having me investigated. It's clear he's having me followed."

"Okay, sorry to hear it, but you were there at the ambassador's invitation, and you'd been in and out of the vault at his invitation. He's going to have a hard time making a case on those facts. Of course—to make a case—he'd have to report the theft. Did he?"

Max's silence answered the question.

"Of course he didn't, because his possession of the Buddha isn't legal. So he can't report it. Which means whoever stole it, has it, end of story. They don't need to implicate anyone else, so the fact they have the video means next to nothing." Which sounded great, but Walter wouldn't see it that way. The Fortunate Buddha still needed to be retrieved and the disc destroyed or she could kiss her IAAR career good-bye.

At this point, she might be kissing it good-bye regardless.

"I am not as worried about the thief as I am the ambassador. If I doubted his intentions before the incident in the park, I don't now. You don't send five armed men for a chat."

"Okay. He's still not going to get me on camera anywhere. I avoided them all. He found me because you found me." Training 101, avoiding surveillance allowed one to come and go without fear of just such a net being cast. She tried not to focus on how the hell he'd found her.

"Oui." He grinned. "I reviewed some of those tapes myself after you vanished. I was most frustrated you were only on one."

Anya froze. He'd found an image of her beyond the one in the vault.

Well, that could be a problem.

"Chérie." Max reached across the table and captured her hand before she could escape. "I will protect you. I do not care about what crimes you have committed in the past. This burden is mine. I put you into this situation, and I will rectify it."

"Wait a minute." She shook her head and turned her hand over so he could brush his thumbs over her palm. "You forget, I was there to retrieve the Buddha. You didn't invite me to the ambassador's ball, you didn't ask me to dance...well, okay you did, but only after I approached you. And you didn't force me to return the Buddha. I'm a big girl. I knew what I did and I knew about the risks."

"All this may be true, but if I hadn't planted the flat cam, you would not have been put into a dangerous position. You would not have entered the party or been associated with me...and as sorry as I am for the distress it may cause you, I am...I am glad for it as well."

"It's fine. Don't worry about it. I can go under for a few months. The heat will blow over. It always does." And if I go deep enough, the heat won't reach me anyway. She could use the time to figure out just who took the Buddha. If she retrieved and presented it to Walter, she could avoid the blacklist. She loved her job. She loved the challenge of the hunt and the acquisition. But, more, she loved reuniting stolen antiquities with their rightful owners. Balancing the scales of past injustices, righting wrongs.

Her missions were her reality.

"Don't dismiss my assistance. I want to help you."

"Why?" The question popped out before she could stop it. All lust aside, why help me?

"Because of me you are in danger. Because, without me, you would have been away from the vault with the Buddha and no one would have been the wiser save for the flat cam." He held up his hand, but his expression arrested her retort. He meant it. He seemed genuinely upset his actions affected her.

"You are in danger because of me, chérie. I would never forgive myself if something happened to you. I have to help you. I assure you, I am capable of a great deal. I am placing myself at your disposal. Use me."

She bit down on the inside of her lip to keep from laughing. She'd always imagined what a knight in shining Armani might say to her someday, but "use me" hadn't made the list.

"I do believe I have used you quite a bit."

"Oui, but I give you carte blanche to use me, use my resources, use my knowledge. But let me make this right—for you."

Her pulse skipped at the fire blazing in his eyes and the hope turning up the corners of his mouth.

"Max. Stop. Please." Humiliating need flash-fire flushed through her, and her pulse thundered in her ears. If desire were a palpable thing, it would press her down to the floor under the leaden weight of emotional cascade all tinged with regret. "This is such an unmitigated disaster."

"Perhaps, but I like to think of it as a fortunate series of events."

"Fortunate? Really? There's optimistic and then there's cuckoo." She twirled her index finger in a circular motion near her forehead.

"Well." He ticked his reasons off on his fingers. "We survived relatively unscathed in the park. We're together. We are working together."

She planted her feet. His last reason sparked irritation with the absolute truth in it and her willingness to fight fled. "Are we?"

"You bit down on the inside of your lip. Your eyes slid just a bit to the right, but you wouldn't look away from me. And your skin...your skin sparkles with lust." The confidence in his words grew with his smile. "You like me, chérie. We are going to be fabulous together."

"Okay, just because I am considering using your resources does not mean we are together." This time the smile escaped her despite biting down hard enough to taste the faint coppery hint of blood.

"Come, sit. Eat. We can discuss everything afterwards."

Anya hesitated, rocking on the balls of her feet. She could go back to the table, or she could just walk out the door. The latter was probably the safer course of action.

She plopped gracelessly into the chair, crossing one bare leg over the other. Her foot tapped the air to a rhythm of the thoughts racing through her mind. Snatching up her fork, she speared a zucchini and pointed the vegetable at him.

She wasn't exactly big on choosing the safer options.

"You shouldn't think winning this argument means you'll always win them."

His smile spread, relaxing the tension in his jaw. Does he have to be so damn handsome? He took her breath away.

"What?"

"Nothing, chérie. Eat." He made a great show of spreading his napkin in his lap once more.

She watched him as she bit into the zucchini. It remained succulent and flavorful even if it had cooled during their discussion. His expression remained pleased, if careful, and she decided to ignore him in favor of the food. Her stomach growled. Ideas prowled around her mind.

"Do you know who stole it?" Anya asked, taking a bite of salmon.

"Non." The reminder of a mutual thorn in their sides dashed away his cat-in-the-cream expression. "But we will find out. I am investigating those who were at the party as well as any who accessed the grounds. They must have slipped in behind us and out just as quickly."

Her expression must have revealed her skepticism because he paused to send her a questioning look.

"It's a great plan, I guess, if you want to spend the next several months on deep background checks, probes, and tape review. But, to be honest, you could do all of it and still come up with too many variables to really factor a suspect."

"You have a better suggestion, chérie?" Challenge filled his voice.

"You find out where the Fortunate Buddha went."

"Pardon?"

"Look, figuring out how the guy—or girl—did it isn't as important as the Buddha itself. I don't really care if our thief was a gymnastic marvel with more gizmos than you find in MI-6. What I care about is where the Buddha went. If you trace the Buddha, you find out who sold it. You find who sold it, well then, you have who took it."

Max stroked his chin. "The plan has possibilities. But many collectors will be like the ambassador—they will not advertise what they are not supposed to own."

"Well, not publicly. But you know the rich and the filthy rich better than anyone. They let people know. They can't help it. They increase security, they purchase display cases, they host an unnecessary event filled with pomp and circumstance because it allows them to show off without really showing off."

"Truly. You seem to have remarkable grasp on the rich and the filthy rich."

"Of course. You're the type of guy I acquire from. It's always smart to know your targets."

"What would you acquire from me?" He picked up his glass of wine, the last of the tension washing away. They were just two lovers sharing a meal in the penthouse suite of a very expensive hotel.

"Whatcha got?" She cocked both brows and waggled them. Okay, so she forgave him. Wow, that didn't take long. The flat cam pissed her off, but he'd come clean. He hadn't tried to blackmail her, and, when they had sex, he'd whispered those sweet endearments into her ear.

They have a word for that, you know. She ignored the strident little voice.

"I have many fine things. But I am not sure I have found a pattern to your acquisitions."

And you won't. She swallowed her food to keep from grinning. The type of work she did for the IAAR was far and above don't show, don't tell. "I like all kinds of things. I'm eclectic."

He chuckled, leaning forward now and closing the gap between them. The air electrified around her, a static charge just waiting to be released. "If you had to choose only one type of acquisition, what would you prefer? Jewels, antiques, rare items...?"

"Hmm, only one?" She mimed a face, lower lip jutting into a pout. "I think it would be a crime to make me choose only one."

"Ah, yet which one is the question. You must choose but one item or one type of item. What do you most hunger for? What can you not live without?"

"Max, I can't answer. I like all of it." Sad, but true. She enjoyed the acquisition of all of the above. She loved the thrill of the hunt, the tension singing through her blood as she made her move, and the pure thrill of victory when she reclaimed an item. It was more, too. She'd seen tears in an old woman's eyes as she reclaimed a painting stolen from her family by the Nazis. The woman sobbed in broken English as a small piece of her innocence and youth returned to her. Emotion clogged Anya's throat.

Returning legacies she'd do for free.

"You are a difficult woman, chérie." He set his wine glass aside and reached for her hand, pausing just out of reach.

"I thought it was the appeal." Every word and action was purposed. Even the lazy demeanor, the bon vivant playboy—he affected it all with purpose. She set aside the fork and slid her hand over into his. He'd asked this time. He'd not demanded or simply grabbed her.

Her heart flip-flopped. He could be so damn sweet.

"You dared me in Prague." He smiled encouragingly, stroking the back of her hand with his thumb.

"Really?" He stroked her with a glance, a tangible caress sending blood rushing to her cheeks.

"Oh yes. I walked into the lounge, bored with the weather and the interminable delays, and a series of meetings were stalling on protocol. And there you were, sitting at the bar, your challenge beckoning me like a Siren calling sailors to the rocks."

A thrill pulsed in her stomach. "Maybe you should have taken the warning."

"I fear I am rather like Odysseus. I don't see warnings, just obstacles to be bested." The statement would have sounded pompous from any other man. "You were intrigued."

"Pretty confident, aren't you?"

"Oui. But you see, after four years, I've made a habit of studying you when we are together. You are not always honest, but you rarely lie. At least not with your body."

She picked up her wine glass and took another swallow, uncomfortable with the direction of the conversation.

"Your mouth, however, weaves taller tales than an Irish bartender after St. Patrick's Day."

"There's probably an insult there, but thank you."

He laughed. "You're welcome. So tell me, Anya with no last name, why the Buddha? What beckoned you to it?"

"It's pure gold." She glanced away as she finished the glass of wine.

"Definitely appealing."

"It's invaluable."

His fingers tightened on her.

"Max...."

"Anya, the Fortunate Buddha is valuable but hardly worth the trouble of traveling to Morocco, countermanding the ambassador's security, and removing it from the country in secret. You wouldn't make enough on the item to justify the risk or the expenditure, not particularly one as hot as the Buddha is now."

"It depends on the buyer. There is far more to the Buddha than the gold."

"The legend?" A smile wound through his words. He squeezed her hand lightly then lifted it to press delicious kisses to each knuckle. "Are you a believer?"

"Hmm, let's see, since I rubbed the Buddha's belly, I've been caught on a flat cam, narrowly escaped a country, been attacked in a park and shot at. Not seeing the good fortune there."

"Ah, glass is half empty. You did see the camera, which prevented you from leaving incriminating evidence behind. You were able to return the Buddha. We eluded our attackers. I see much good fortune." Amusement warmed every word.

"Do you always look for the positive?"

"Do you always look for the negative?"

She dropped her attention to the table, to the meal remnants between them, the picture of normalcy. "Your ambassador is unlikely to give up easily, Max. You have the wealth and the connections. Perhaps you should use them." The words no sooner left her lips than she realized he would never do it. He was a hell of a lot more than surface polish.

As expected, he ignored the comment. "You should plan on staying with me for a few days."

"Days?"

"Days. Until we locate the Buddha or the thief who took him. It will be safer for you to stay with me." It wasn't a question. He punctuated his sentence with a kiss to her hand.

"Not to point out the flaw in your logic but you're the big kahuna where the ambassador is concerned. He didn't find me. You did."

"Oui. But his men have seen you now, and you can bet they have your photograph. With enough effort, they can and will find you."

Ah hell. Walter's gonna kill me. "I appreciate the concern, I do. But I'll be fine. I'm also more likely to find the Buddha without you hanging around my neck."

"You left in Prague. You lied to me in Florence. You escaped in Paris. Rabat was the first time you trusted me. You're not going anywhere without me."

The implied threat should have frightened her, or at least warned her off, but a warm, wanted feeling unfurled in her belly. She rose, tugging her hand free to walk over to the windows. Sprawling around them were the canyons of London's ancient, twisting streets.

"Your ambassador friend. He wanted the Fortunate Buddha and was likely willing to do anything to get it." The gunshots in the park suggested a willingness to do whatever it took to punish them, Buddha or not.

"Henri is a taciturn man and set in his ways, but I can hardly imagine he is willing to kill. He will cool off, eventually."

"Will he?" In six years of service to the IAAR, Anya had numerous run-ins with all types of free agents and mercenaries, all out for a profit for themselves, but willing to do whatever it took, even putting a bullet in her if it meant they got the treasure and she didn't.

It wasn't all simple acrobatics and chicanery. In fact, often times it was a lot more than both. The IAAR took such a careful hand in profiling her jobs before she went on them, and when they expected serious resistance, a team would back her up.

"I see your point, chérie." He joined her at the window, meeting her gaze in the reflection, his expression still. "Perhaps you should let me do the investigation. I will keep you safe until I clear your name."

"You are so sweet." She turned and stroked her knuckles down his cheek. "And it's so not going to happen."

Chapter Eight

The next week took up a pattern. They switched hotels regularly. Max always chose. He used subsidiaries to pay for them and never let her out of his sight. They spent their time making love and researching the Fortunate Buddha. They tapped into their resources, but the idol remained stubbornly out of sight and off the radar. She might have grown frustrated with the hunt, except they'd made a game out of chasing down dead ends.

His appetites for good sex and good food were insatiable. He also seemed intent on spoiling her rotten. When he wasn't seducing her on the bed, on the floor, in the shower, or at the desk, he bought her clothes and ordered in exotic meals.

Through it all, she steadfastly refused to return to her own apartment. Her purse, her cell phone, and an ID card were enough. She'd made a point of hiding her card because, beyond their search for the Buddha, he wanted her name.

Her full name.

She enjoyed his attempts to get at it, such as now, when she lay naked and panting, his fingers and mouth turning her insides to putty. He would bring her to the brink, stroking firmly, and then hold off her pleasure and ask her.

Anticipation curled through her sex. His thumb glided between her labia, stroking the length of her slick entrance. Pressure swelled in her clit, pressure he refused to appease as he continued the slow, lazy petting.

"Do you like that?"

The sensations blooming inside of her were edgy, desperate. "Yes." The word cut out of her, her hips jerking up as though to force his hand where she wanted him. But he pushed his palm downward, a glide by, which left her aching.

"Tell me your name."

"Anya." She panted, barely able to smile around the grit of her teeth. She ground her ass to the sheets, only slightly better than shoving her pelvis up to him and begging.

"Full name." He dipped a finger into her and pressed along the roof of her sex. She shot her hand down to grab his, desperate to take what he denied, but he resisted her. When her own fingers sought her aching clit, he slapped them away and laughed.

Still, she held onto the information, refusing to give in to the craving of her body. When he slipped up over her, a lock of hair fell over his forehead, and her heart did another of those strange somersaults. He shackled the wrist of her offending hand in his and pressed it up against the bed. She arched, offering him her breasts, and her thighs softened as she strained for the last refused caress.

"Tell me," he commanded in a low, husky voice with his accent pronounced.

"No. Not today." She hissed out a breath as he caught one nipple, laving it with his tongue and suckling at the sensitive tip. Her nails sank into his shoulders as he held himself above her, his cock replacing his fingers to tease her slick entrance.

Exasperation and adoration mingled in his sigh, and she saw her moment. Sliding her legs up along the back of his thigh, she hooked them over his hips and squeezed. He drove home in one thrust, and rushed the orgasm to completion.

His groan vibrated her breast. "Chérie, you are terrible."

His weight shifted, but soon his strokes became firmer, harder, and deeper. She rocked her hips up to meet him, clinging to him as he drove her over the edge, and she spiraled only to hear his shout as he followed.

Every day offered a new adventure. Her fierce independence attracted and frustrated him. She lay on her side, the sheet tangled around her hips. Every day they made love and reached for pleasure he hadn't thought possible. In the past, his affairs had always been very short, a night or two spread out over a few weeks.

Never longer.

Never enough to allow my lovers to become attached.

Yet, he lay here, watching her sleep. He ran a finger down the slender shoulder to the tiny, compact body with its hidden delights that continued to fascinate him. He was growing attached.

Too attached.

Pietr had accused him of as much in their phone call the night before, and they had no leads on the Buddha. Worse, he was no closer to discovering more about her.

He knew she preferred her coffee black, when she drank it, but favored hot tea. She disdained herbal blends and red wines. She liked fish better than steak. She preferred her showers hot and her sex hotter. She surrendered control to him and enjoyed turning the tables to take what she wanted.

He'd woken up more than once to her mouth on him, his sleep dissolving in a tidal wave of pleasure. The way her mind worked fascinated him. How she focused so doggedly on their search and ducked all of his personal questions.

He'd yet to send Pietr her fingerprints. Pietr wanted to know why. He'd demanded to know. Max continued to put him off. The insistent electronic buzz of his cell phone cut across his thoughts. He stretched across her and picked it up, flipping it open before it woke her.

"Oui?"

"I have a lead for you." Pietr's brusque tone said he was still peeved.

"The Buddha?"

"Yes. It would appear that du Monde is shopping it in Geneva."

The bastard Frenchman stole it? "Order the plane made ready. Anya and I will be on our way shortly."

"You are bringing her?"

"Pietr," he warned him.

"You are a fool, Maxwell. She is a thief."

"Yes, we all have our crosses to bear, Cousin. Now, have the plane made ready."

"I will expect six months free use of your chalet in the Alps."

"Yes, yes." He laughed. Pietr rarely continued a battle he wasn't sure he could win, and he rarely won when Max truly wanted something. He rang off without another word. He flipped the phone closed and studied Anya. Dark lashes flickered up, revealing the twin gray clouds, which gazed at him languidly.

"Good morning. What's wrong?" She peered at him, the sleep fading from her.

He considered withholding the information, dragging out the pleasure for as long as it would last. He wanted honesty from her. He wanted her trust. He wanted her confidence. To earn it, he had to return it.

"We have a lead on the Buddha."

Excitement bunched her muscles as she bounced off the bed. "All right. It's about time. When do we leave, and do I have time for a shower?"

"Absolument. The plane is being made ready. We are heading to Geneva. You will need your passport. Take your shower, and we can go to the airport."

"Got it. We'll have to stop at the bank on the way." She clenched her fists, nearly skipping as she approached, then threw her arms around him and kissed him hard. "A lead is excellent. I can't wait to nail the son of a bitch who set us up."

"Oui." But for some reason, his heart wasn't in it. She didn't seem to notice as she twirled away, leaving him holding only the air.

"We'll have the Buddha, our thief, the video, and our freedom— I can taste it." She snapped her fingers and vanished into the bathroom.

He watched her, swallowing his own regret. "Damn fool."

"What?" she called from the bathroom, the water turning on.

"Nothing," he answered. "Just muttering to myself."

Her head peeked around the door, beckoning. "You are going to join me, right?"

"Oh, oui." Abandoning his dark thoughts, he strode for her and the shower.

A private car carried them to the airstrip where they boarded a private plane. The plush accommodations were as welcome as they were unfamiliar. She sank into the white seat during takeoff, fixed on the chiseled line of Max's jaw where a muscle ticked. He stared out the window, watching London fade away below them.

Is he regretting his choices? Is he plotting some other trick? As much as she believed he meant no harm, he had planted the flat cam. She tried to reconcile the man who'd planted the camera and tracked her down with the man who'd held her tenderly for the last week.

The sigh escaped confinement before she could stop it.

"It will be fine, chérie." His teeth flashed white with a smile, one that failed to reach his eyes. "We will secure the Buddha and the disc footage from the flat cam."

"Actually, I'm really not worried about it. If Louis were going to do anything with the disc, he would have done it by now." The moment she spoke the words, she wanted to take them back. His expression arrested and shuttered. His jaw clenched, and his lips compressed. She glimpsed a fleeting bleakness in his expression before his face smoothed.

"Yes, you and Viscount du Monde share a history." The words were hollow points, loaded with an indefinable emotion.

"It wasn't important." She fought the urge to squirm.

"It is not every day I have a woman breathless from my kisses who whispers another man's name in my ear." His tight smile was anything but friendly, as if the bitter sting had occurred the night before and not on some empty night years before.

"Max...."

He cut her off with a sharp wave of his hand. "I really do not wish to walk down that particular lane again. You were lovers. I can accept your history. I do not have to like it. You are not still lovers." While he said the last without the intimation of a question, his gaze sharpened on her face. She could practically feel the speculation raging within him.

"We are not, no."

"I imagine the breakup was not mutual, for you were avoiding him at the ambassador's." Again, he sought confirmation for his statement, and she nodded. She could hardly explain her relationship with Louis, as convoluted as her assignments from the IAAR. He'd been an asset, one they'd tested for possible use in the field and one who bit them like an ill-tempered dog.

She'd earned more than one scar from the experience.

"Louis maintains a home in Geneva." Apparently, he'd moved on from the discussion of their past. "He is most likely keeping the Buddha there. I have someone working on the plans and the specifications. My pilot will make our landing arrangements at the last moment, and we will be using an airfield in Chêne-Bougeries. It is an older airstrip dating from the Second World War and used primarily by evacuees. I have an old friend who maintains it for historical purposes. While it is not an active field, it is suitable for landing and only six kilometers from Geneva. It will be sufficient to delay the ambassador's bloodhounds."

"Is it going to be far enough? I mean, we're running on a lot of speculation. We're not even sure Louis took the Fortunate Buddha."

"Non, we are not." He dropped the pretense and leaned forward, long, tapered fingers capturing her hand and cradling it between his own. "Anya, I meant it when I said I would do everything in my power to protect you. You are right, we are not sure du Monde has the Buddha or the disc, but he is our best lead. He has reasonable motive. He has reasonable history with us both."

"You can't stand him."

He bit out another ferocious grin. "Non."

"May I ask why?" She couldn't resist the probing.

"Oui." The tempestuous storm of emotion in him receded. "You can ask, but you must offer me something in exchange."

"We're bartering?" Intrigued in spite of herself, she swallowed a laugh. He continued to surprise her with his choices, his actions, and his words. After a week spent indulging her senses, she should have built up some immunity to him, but her heart did a little flip-flop in her chest, and her lungs burned with the scent of him.

"Oh, oui. We didn't stop bartering. Now I want an even exchange going forward. Information for information."

"I see." Anya fought the smile tugging at her lips. The gulf between them shrank to the table, bridged where his fingers laced through hers. "So one answer for another."

"Oui." The gleam in his eyes chased away the shadows. "Will you play with me?"

She bit down hard on the inside of her lip, the closest she could come to pinching herself and not feel foolish. He didn't disappear, however, so her smile grew. The sting of the bite reminded her of reality.

"All right. I'll play, but you go first."

Any doubts skittered away under the dazzling smile he gave her. He squeezed her hands and let her go, his thumb caressing the side of her palm, arousing a longing for him to take her hands again. "Very well. Louis and I were mates at Eton and again at Cambridge, although he lapsed for a year when he attended Harvard in Massachusetts."

"I know where Harvard is." She gave into her laughter, settling in to listen. She loved it when his voice abandoned the French rhythm for a more clipped British tone. In fact, his syntax was her next question—why did he favor the French to the British?

"Very well," he mocked her almost playfully. "We've always been a bit competitive. It increased during Cambridge, particularly after I cracked the security on his home to retrieve some papers he'd lifted from one of our professors."

"He stole from the instructors?"

"More like borrowed, or so he claimed, in order to facilitate a more advantageous grade."

"He cheated."

"Oh, oui. He also treated a girl of mine rather badly, so I thought one foul turn deserved another."

"So you took some papers?"

Max opened one bottle of water and offered her another bottle. "Oui, and replaced them with a different set."

Anya burst out laughing. "Did he fail?"

"Oh. Oui." Masculine satisfaction whistled through the word. "It cost him a great deal to stay in the program, and he's never quite forgiven me."

"I can see you're terribly contrite."

He shrugged, but the smile playing with his lips threatened to devastate her with its charm. "My turn."

She sucked in a deep breath, nervousness tumbling through her belly in ripples of anticipation. "Give it your best shot."

"Why do you want the Fortunate Buddha?"

"Wow." She blinked. The question came from so far afield she wasn't even sure what direction it traveled to get onto the topic of conversation.

"An answer for an answer, chérie."

"I know. I just wasn't expecting that question." She couldn't resist smiling in answer to his pleased grin. He obviously enjoyed surprising her. So, how much information could she give him? She tugged at her ear, thinking.

Truth.

Yeah. The best route.

She really didn't want to lie to him.

"I was hired to get it."

Max paused, water bottle tilted for a drink as he searched her expression. She felt a twinge of satisfaction for being the one who startled him this time.

"Really?"

"Yes. I said a job. The Buddha was taken from a temple in northern Thailand a few years ago. It passed from private collector to private collector. The monks could never afford much, and they never prevented anyone from visiting or touching the Buddha. They just want it returned."

"So, you work for these monks, then?" He angled forward, his elbows returning to the table, thoughts whirling in his mind pulsing the air around them.

"That's two questions, and it's my turn."

"So it is, chérie. So it is. Very well. Ask your question."

"Why did you plant the flat cam?" She nearly hesitated to ask the question. It begged danger and disagreement. Her stomach ached at the thought of all the reasons why he would have wanted to trap her. He'd told her some of it in the hotel room, but it didn't make sense.

His smile eased away, caution taking its place. She hoped it meant good things and not the bad things that made her stomach flutter like a herd of wild nerves on the loose. "I told you why I did it."

"Tell me again. Tell me all of it, and I promise I won't go ballistic like I did at the hotel."

"All right." He sighed and closed the water bottle before reaching over to capture her hands again. She didn't want to be touching him during the story. She wanted to keep her good judgment in place. She considered withdrawing, but the contact sent electricity skittering up her arms. The hair on her nape stood up as he stroked his thumbs over the pulse points on her wrists.

Was it fear, passion, or some heady combination of the two turning her judgment to mush?

A wordless play of emotions scampered across her features. He was certain if she had any idea of how much of an open book she acted, she'd jerk away from him for sure. As it was, he could see she fought the urge to abandon his grasp.

He could admire the emotion, but he wanted the touch. He wanted her to feel him when he told her this. He wanted to feel the pulse leaping beneath his thumbs.

"I wanted to get to know you." He chose the words carefully. "From the first time we met, I wanted you. But you were always disappearing on me. You were always just out of reach. I thought.... Hell, I don't know what I thought. I wanted to see you in action. I wanted to see what you could do. Now I want you to ask me if it was the first time I planted a flat cam."

Her throat convulsed as she swallowed, the tiniest candle of hope within her gaze. "It's not my turn."

"Do you want to ask me if it was the first time I planted a camera?"

"Yes."

"Now it's your turn." Max held her focus, refusing to look anywhere but at her. They were the only two people in the entire world, right now, aboard this plane, flying across Europe in pursuit of a mutual goal, but he honestly could have cared less about it. He liked imagining she felt the same way.

"Was it the first time you planted a flat cam"—Anya hesitated, her hands tightening under his, pulse leaping—"to look for me?"

God, he loved how her mind worked. She made the leap with so little prompting. His heart ached. "No. I've been planting them since our last rendezvous in Paris."

"The collector's book."

"Oui. You left me aching then, luv. Aching with want, aching with need. Aching for you. I've been leaving those cameras on every job I did, hoping for just a glimpse, even the smallest one. I am sorry finding it in the ambassador's vault gave you such a fright, but I will never be sorry it brought you to me."

"Wow."

He adored her single-syllable response. Her tiny white teeth dragged over her lower lip. He held still to keep from reaching across and claiming her mouth with his own.

"You're crazy." Thankfully, laughter softened the words, but she was pleased. He could see it in the pink flush to her cheeks and the way her fingers curled into his palms, nails grazing lightly.

"Perhaps. But I am a very happy man at the moment."

"It's a shame it has to end. You worked so hard."

"End?" Everything inside of him went still.

"Yeah. We're going to get Louis, get the disc, get the Buddha, and that will be that—obligation discharged." She glanced at their joined hands.

"Of course." The words turned to ash against his tongue. "Obligation discharged."

"Max." His name slipped off her lips, soft and inviting.

He dragged his gaze over her face and saw the uncertainty reflecting back at him. "Anya?"

"How long until we land?"

Impatient, he twisted his arm to glance at his watch but refused to let go of the hands he held, hands that would be going with her when they parted from their obligation. He tried not to spit the word out again.

"Another hour, at least."

"Wonderful." Something arch in her voice kicked his heart.

"Oh?"

She stood, swung around the table and onto his lap. His body stirred with an immediate response, and he slid his fingers up, cupping her nape as she sank into him for a kiss. With one hand, he reached to the panel and depressed a single button alerting the pilot and stewardess not to disturb them.

She tasted of the strawberries, coffee, and sweet cream they'd eaten for breakfast. She opened to his tongue and combed her fingers through his hair. "Max," she murmured again, his name a vibration on her lips.

"Yes?" He shifted, standing and carrying her to the sofa. She wore far too many clothes.

"Thank you."

He hesitated and lifted his head to meet her passion-drenched look. "For making love to you?"

"No. Well, yes, that, too." She laughed, and the sound poured through him. He tugged loose her belt and sent it flying; the shoes, skirt, and shirt followed. Creamy breasts wrapped in tiny bits of black lace filled his vision, and he groaned despite trying to listen to her.

She tapped his chin. "Up here."

He grinned, a lock of hair falling down into his field of vision. "Oh, oui, I want to look at all of you."

"But I want to say this." She hesitated then began to unbutton his shirt while he shrugged out of the suit jacket. "Thank you for setting the flat cam."

He froze, his cock straining between them. "You were angry." It wasn't a question.

"I was." She agreed. "But I'm not anymore. I'm glad."

"Why?" He wanted to know. He needed to know why.

"Because I would never have come to you otherwise...you scare the hell out of me. You scared me in Prague, and you really terrified me in Paris." The low-voiced admission cost her. Capturing her face in his hands, he studied the cascade of emotions racing across her eyes. Tenderness blunted the edges of his temper.

"Why would I frighten you, chérie?"

"Because I've never felt the way I do when I'm with you. It's intoxicating, and it's terrifying, and it's wonderful, and it's intimidating—"

He silenced her with a kiss. His heart kicked his conscience, but he ignored it. He stroked her through the creamy black silk of her blouse. He brushed the bottom of her breast languidly. The little catch in her throat invited more, and he aimed higher, exploring the peak of her nipple through the layers of clothing. His body roared, his self-control at odds with the violent need to take her, possess her, and keep her.

As she began to writhe over him, her sweet little ass rubbing against the tenting of his cock, he watched the fear and tension drain from her expression. Her lips parted, pink tongue just barely peeking out between her teeth. She pumped her hips forward, her face darkening with a storm of longing he recognized. His heart punched into his ribs.

He wanted her. He wanted to taste all her emotion. He wanted to taste her.

He wanted it all.

And the craving terrified him.

Chapter Nine

"It's a great idea."

"It's a terrible idea."

She glared at him, her hands on her hips and arms akimbo as he dismissed her plan with one wave of his hand. "What's terrible about it?"

"Everything. We do this together."

"This is doing it together."

"Anya, no."

Breath hissing out past her teeth, she counted to ten and then to twenty and finally resorted to counting backward in French to get her temper under control. Their hotel room in Geneva was as opulent, if not more, than the one they'd occupied in London. Apparently, Max didn't stay in anything less than six star accommodations.

"We will find another way," he continued, his tone a mixture of patience and determination with just the right amount of calm.

"If he's shopping the Buddha, then we have a day or two at best. You know. You know as well as I do as soon as it leaks, it's nearly over and done with. For all you know, that party tonight could be his private auction. Our best chance at getting into his files, his vaults and finding what we need is tonight, while he is distracted. And who is better at distraction than I am?"

The laptop slammed closed. A muscle twitched in his cheek. Apparently, even his patience could be cracked if struck with an Anya-sized mallet. "Is this about the Buddha, or do you just want to see Louis again?"

"What?"

Long, tapered fingers tapped the top of the laptop. An inscrutable expression took up residence on his face. If not for the jerking muscle in his jaw, she might have thought him calm. "If you want to see Louis again, it can wait until this is done and you're safe. I do not trust him, and no matter what your relationship prior to this, you shouldn't trust him either—something I thought we both agreed on in Rabat."

Quiet, contained rage shimmered in the air between them. Her mind went into overdrive.

"I am sorry if your previous lovers had no problems with you visiting an ex before, I am not one of those." He rose, stalking across the room and invading her space. The coiled energy in the air vibrated over her skin. She barely had time to process before Max wrapped his arms around her and trapped her against the hardness of his body. "We will do this together, Anya."

Tread carefully.

The thoughtfully snarky little voice didn't care for the quiet danger drifting through the forest of his eyes. "We are doing this together." She kept the pitch of her voice soft, but serious. "You need time to access his systems, to crack his codes, to get inside. You need the security of knowing he's tied up and not likely to intrude on what you're doing. I can give you the time. It's a party for the arts center, and there are going to be hundreds of people there."

"A week ago, you didn't want to see him, and now you do." He scowled. "I don't want you anywhere near him."

"What's he going to do? Bite me?" Her lips quirked into a half-smile. Sliding her hands up the smooth, rich Egyptian cotton of his dark-gray shirt, she could feel the thump of his heart as it boxed a one-two-punch interval on his ribs. "I'm just going to be a very good distraction."

"And if Louis is looking for you?" he countered. "If he does indeed have the disc as we suspect, then he knows you were in the vault, he knows you wanted the Buddha. Seeing you there could tip him off."

"Maybe. But I doubt it. Louis is cocky and self-assured. He'll likely want to take advantage of what he presumes is a hold over me."

The color in Max's lips vanished as they descended into a single line slashing across the granite of his expression. "And it doesn't worry you?"

She shrugged. "It didn't bother me when you wanted twelve hours in your bed to help me."

Her only warning to the imminent eruption brewing inside of

him was his harsh, swift inhalation. But his anger was a thing to behold. His jaw locked, and his nostrils flared. The dark coloring of his hair enhanced the deeper tan of his skin. He would have been at home in the wilds of the Celtic landscape, blue paint splattered along one side of his finely chiseled features, a battle axe in hand.

"You will not forget that particular statement, will you?"

"Nope, probably not, especially if you keep going all caveman on me. I am who I am. Getting the Buddha back, securing the disc are really my problem. I love how you want to help me. You came to me, you warned me, and we're here together. But you don't get to dictate the how, the what, and the when. Not when I can help, and I'm effective at what I do." Bleakness pierced the dark anger, and she dug her fingers into his shirt. "Max, I need you to trust me to do this."

Eyes closed, Max pressed his forehead to hers. Something crackled inside her chest, a rusty chain barricading her heart snapped, releasing a rush of emotion. Her hands slid up his chest to wrap around his neck, and she hugged him tightly.

"I do not like this plan." His words muffled at her throat as he held her even more firmly against him.

"It's not a bad plan. It will take you an hour? Maybe two to get through his system?" She tried to cajole, to coax, to comfort.

"Thirty minutes," he growled. "Less."

"Ooo, now look who's cocky." She tipped her head, trying to read his face, and he lifted his chin with a show of reluctance.

"You will go nowhere with him. You will not let yourself be alone with him. You will break his arm if he tries to touch you."

"I think I can manage that." Hoping for a smile in return, she let the corner of her mouth quirk upward. "I'm pretty mean when I'm angry."

"I'm counting on it." He blew out another breath. "You should shop then if you will be going to the party, and I will get the plans together."

"Max?"

"Yes, luv?"

"Thank you for trusting me."

He paused, staring at her for a long time, and she couldn't fathom what went through his mind. His knuckles brushed down her cheek, and his sad smile twisted her heart. "I want to trust you. I am going to trust you. But I do not like the thought of you near your ex-lover."

Anya began to speak, but he touched his fingers to her lips, silencing her. "Enough for now. Let me focus so this sacrifice will be worth it. I will have a driver take you to the shops you will need."

She nodded slowly and pressed her palm to her lips, still feeling his touch as he walked away.

Her ex-lover.

So many little lies.

Would she ever be able to undo them all?

Later, she promised herself, she promised Max, silently. Later she would make everything right.

"Are you sure these are the right orders?" Max's fingers flew over the keyboard. The Linux window he used revealed layer upon layer of complex coding. He only needed to find the right "if-then" statement to create the tunnel he wanted.

"Oui." Pietr's reply carried the chill of impatience. The wireless headset did little to mask his cousin's displeasure. "Da. Si. You've asked me three times, Maxwell. Each time I have confirmed those machines, the code, and the installation are what the viscount ordered over the last six months. It is the most up-to-date design and security system."

He cursed.

***

The glitz and the glamour at the Grand Theatre de Geneva appeared far more conservative than the ambassador's New Year's Eve party in Rabat just a few short days before. Where the clothing left little to the imagination, Geneva's snowy landscape invited fur-lined capes, hoods with ermine trim, and more ice dripping from the women than from the rooftops.

She didn't stand out in the deep-chocolate dress with the velvet bodice and gold filigree lacing. Max had nearly swallowed his tongue when she'd walked out of the bedroom, the plunging neckline and backless dress having invited more than a few comments from him.

After all, she was supposed to be a distraction. His grumble about her lack of red shoes made her laugh. The gold sandals were better for this type of work. The heels would snap off with very little effort, and the lace bindings snaking up her calves meant the shoes would stay on if she needed to run.

Hopefully, not through snow, though.

After ordering a flute of ginger ale, she began the slow mingle. She'd taken note of Louis the moment she entered the room. He chatted with several other guests on the far side of the room while sipping from a tumbler, of cognac, no doubt.

Nothing but the finest for the Viscount du Monde.

She continued her measured stroll of the room, pausing at the different clusters of people. She met, smiled, and murmured greetings. Parties like this were about being seen as much as they were about mingling and networking. Her route took her slowly toward her oblivious quarry.

The crowd parted as she moved on, and Louis looked up, his predatory gaze trailing across the room to lock with her own. The spark of recognition shuddered across his features and, she hoped, tripped up his words. Nice to have such a profound effect on a member of the opposite sex.

Particularly this pompous jackass.

She took a sip of ginger ale to mask her smile as he withdrew from his conversation and hastened across the crowd to her. His fellow bluebloods hampered his progress. Anya let him pursue, engaging an older man in an ambassadorial sash with a wink.

Louis wasn't without his charms. He was tall, even handsome, with simple but memorable features. His rust-colored hair gave him a burnished appearance under the warm incandescent lights of the opera house. He wore his tuxedo the way some men wore blue jeans and T-shirts. But the easiness of his bearing and manner evaporated at his cold, dead eyes. They were pale, too pale, like chips of ice stolen away to cap his otherwise inviting landscape with a snowy peak.

"Ahhhnya." He exhaled her name then fell into step beside her. The hairs on her body stood at attention as apprehension slithered over her skin.

"Louis." She paused and executed the perfect pivot, favoring him with a winsome smile. "Louis du Monde, it has been far too long."

"Has it?" His brows rose in challenge as he leaned in to brush a kiss to each cheek. His lips were cold and stiff on her skin. He captured her free hand in his own then lifted it to his lips, pausing to breathe the words across the surface of her knuckles. "I do believe it was just a couple of weeks ago...or less."

"Was it?" Airy smile. Keep it light. Keep it even. "I am sorry. I don't recall."

"Rabat. The French ambassador's New Year's Eve party. I saw you dancing with Sauvage, you naughty tease." His chiding bordered on condescension, but something moved behind the glacial front, something dangerous peeking out.

"Ahh. I wasn't at the party long, and Max demanded a great deal of my time." She tried to mimic the pout favored by the other women, but it wasn't her thing. She took another sip of her ginger ale and tried to extract her hand, but Louis held it with determination.

Bastard.

"You know, I still remember our night in Paris."

"Another near miss? Who was I dancing with then?" She focused on Louis, blotting out the room around them. She wanted his attention on her. She wanted him away from other contacts. Max needed this time.

He would have it.

"So provocative. You play the game well, but you should know, I do not play to lose."

"Why would anyone play to lose?"

"Some play larger hands than they can afford to lose because they believe gambling is about the risk and not the gain."

"Gambling is about risk and gain. Loss just happens to be a fact of both." Anya tugged her hand ever so slightly, but Louis only smiled and turned, taking her captured hand and sliding it through his arm, laying his hand over it, and holding it hostage. Walk or risk a scene if she forced him to drag her.

"Only amateurs believe in factoring in the loss. The true expert knows it is about winning. The risks are layered in to achieve the maximum goal. If you play for anything less, then you deserve to lose." They resumed her sedate stroll through the grand gallery, but she spied an exit on the far side. An exit leading to another part of the opera house, and Louis led them both toward it.

"Risk is about conflict. Conflicts can be overcome or sacrificed. It really depends on whether the gain is ultimately worth it." A spare glance at the diamond watch on her wrist revealed they were well and truly past the thirty-minute mark and no word from Max.

She really hoped his estimate was correct.

"Anya." Louis dipped his head down, invading her space with an intimacy she didn't share. "Why are you here?"

"I heard you were selling something which belongs to me."

"Oh?"

"Oh."

They were approaching the exit, and her heart jumped, straining with her effort to not jerk herself away. "And what item are you referring to, my lovely Siren?"

The door loomed ahead of them; she hoped for a lock, a hope which shattered when a youngish looking man in serving livery opened the door for their approach. Like Max, Louis was loaded, and loaded meant oodles of influence.

She would be alone with Louis a lot sooner than she'd anticipated. Louis guided her through the door with one hand on the bare skin of her lower back and the other on her still captive hand.

Should have worn the blue dress. It came with a bigger purse, and her Taser fit nicely into it.

"You're welcome."

Derivative of Richard Pace's work, the system's organic code continually rewrote pieces of itself with an encrypted algorithm. It would revert to the access codes if given the correct sequencing, which Max could find with a backdoor. But after nearly two hours of code dancing, his nerves were fraying to the breaking point.

He'd told her thirty minutes.

They were ninety minutes past deadline.

He swore again, ignoring Pietr's grunt on the other end of the phone. His cousin handled web searches, information pulls, and other miscellaneous work while Max took care of the actual job. He worked from inside his car, less than a block from the viscount's Geneva estate.

She was at the Royal Opera Hall with Louis.

After lifting his fingers from the keyboard, he clenched his hands. Jealousy was not a comfortable emotion. It gnawed at his insides with a thousand tiny bites, shredding his concentration and confidence.

"Max?"

"Oui?"

"We may have a problem. This second set of orders includes an independent, self-contained system on property. It has no networking capabilities."

He paused. "Any other specs on file?"

"No." The single syllable carried a weight of worry.

Reading the code in front of him, he spotted the problem. Trojan horse. "Shut it down, Pietr. This is not something I can do remotely."

"Well, you're not going in there."

"Not right now." He yanked out the cable and shut down the satellite card. He'd recorded enough data on the code. He would work it tonight. "Send me the alternative specs."

"You're a code breaker, not a break and enterer."

"De rien, Pietr." Max hung up and started the car. He was already in a suit and tie, but he needed to get in, get his woman, and get out without Louis noticing.

He dialed the disposable cell phone he'd given her earlier, but when she didn't answer, he pressed down on the pedal a little harder.

She crossed one leg over the other and kept watch on Louis across the table. He'd chosen a secluded little room off the main ballroom, ordered up food and wine despite her protests.

"My offer is still on the table." He smiled, using the silver to cut away a piece of tender lamb served in a mint sauce. "You've never answered my proposition."

"Come to work for you or be your mistress?"

"Both."

"I think I'll decline." She rotated her ankle, glancing at her watch. She'd avoided the wine in favor of water and barely nibbled at the salad. Thankfully, Louis was content to talk, but, after two hours, she was starting to worry. What if Max had been caught? What if he'd managed to get in?

What if he'd already managed to get the disc or the Buddha? Or both?

She shifted and tried to block out the niggling, nagging doubts. When had he given her any reason to doubt him?

His indecent proposal?

He wanted me. He helped me even when I didn't agree.

His planting the flat cam in the first place?

He wanted to know more about me.

His hunting you down in London even after you covered your tracks?

He wanted to help me.

The doubts ate away at her insides, twisting her stomach into knots and leaving the salad she'd consumed earlier sitting like a hard lump.

"You seem troubled."

"I'm actually just waiting for you to get to the point. You swooped in, dragged me in here for a private supper, and reminded me of a proposition you made two years ago. I'm really just not sure why it's important to you."

"Does it really confuse you so much?" His expression betrayed a cynical amusement, a twisted parody of Max's devilish charm and playful manner. "After all, Sauvage can barely keep his hands to himself where you're concerned. Why should I be any different? I assure you, our wealth is comparable, and I know of your lust for adventure. I've followed your exploits quite closely."

The earlier chill of apprehension frosted her spine.

"Your technique is amazing, and your physical control is astonishing. I could use you in so many ways." His emphasis on use boiled the bits away from the hard lump in her stomach, leaving it a churning mass of illness.

Time to go.

"I'm not really sure I know what you mean by use, or if I want to know what you mean." Anya stood, depositing her napkin on the uneaten food in front of her. "But I'm not for sale."

Louis rose with her, sliding around the table with a speed she wouldn't have expected. His hands came to rest on her shoulders, fingers biting into the flesh with a warning.

"Everyone is for sale."

"I'm not."

He smiled. With one hand, she reached to push him away as his head descended and those cold, hard lips pressed hers with insult. He jerked her to him, his holding hers captive. She squirmed, pushing his chest, and picked up her foot to slam it down when he vanished suddenly.

Louis' laughter echoed in her ears as she stared into Max's blazing fury.

Oh no.

Chapter Ten

"**M**ax." Her breathy whisper wrapped around the syllable of his name and flattened the naked anger roaring through him. She'd been in Louis' arms. He'd seen her try to push him away, and he'd seen her pick up her foot. She hadn't wanted to be in Louis' arms, but the bastard had touched her nonetheless.

Rage screamed in his ears, and he held up a single finger to quiet her. He needed to focus on Louis. The source of his ire picked himself up from the floor, dusted his pants off, and smirked.

"Maxwell." The insult condensed around Louis' use of his full name. "How pleasant to see you again. Anya and I were just discussing you." He enjoyed himself.

At Max's expense.

At Anya's expense.

He took a step forward, and a slender hand slid around his upper arm, squeezing him through his suit jacket.

"Max." She said his name, softer this time, her slender frame pressing along his back, but she stayed clear of his arm. She wouldn't be in the way if he cold cocked the smirk right off Louis' face. He would thank her for the wisdom in the gesture later.

He'd never considered himself a violent man. In fact, he favored the indirect, calm approach to the more brutal fisticuffs of others. Still, his blood hummed with the need to feel bone crunching on bone.

"I could tell." Proud of his even tone. "You'll excuse us, Louis. The lady is not feeling well, and I thought we might take a walk."

"But of course." Louis spread his arms wide. "Always the gentleman."

"I am as I was raised to be." He clenched his hand closed and then forcibly released the fingers one by one. He could see the swing—he'd bring up his left, and, when Louis shied away, he'd jab with his right. The hard thrust of his knuckle would dislocate the center knuckle, but the reward would be the cracking of Louis' two hundred thousand dollar nose job to repair Max's previous donation to the Louis du Monde expression.

The air crackled between them, and she squeezed his arm again, interrupting the circuit of vengeful thoughts.

"Shall we go?" she asked in a soft, almost unfamiliar tone. She kept it low key and probably hoped to get them both out of there without a fight.

Yes. He wanted her out of there.

"Yes, we shall." He shifted, moving bodily between where she would move and where Louis stood. Using his hand on the small of her back, he nudged her along to the door and then opened it. "Ahh, one moment."

He turned and swung. As expected, Louis smirked into the dodge and met Max's right uppercut square in the jaw. The nose job wouldn't be disturbed, but a faint crunch of bone and the resounding of clacked teeth echoing the pain searing his knuckles offered a satisfying conclusion to the liquid fury rolling through his veins.

Louis crumpled.

"Holy cr—" Anya gaped at him.

"He always had a glass jaw." He rescued some ice from the bucket on the table and wrapped it around his knuckles with a borrowed cloth napkin before tucking the bloodied fist into his pocket and out of sight.

Stepping over Louis with less notice than he would give to the dog sleeping on the rug, he jerked his head to the bank of doors along the right leading to the lobby and out of the opera house. "We should go."

"Max."

He paused. "No. We will not discuss this here. We will go. We can discuss this later."

Rebellion flashed in her eyes, her mouth compressed, and the slender column of her throat showed the pulse leaping beneath the skin. He stared at her levelly. They did not have time for a dispute in the middle of the Grand Theatre de Geneva with hundreds to bear witness. They needed to leave, quietly, unassumingly, and long before Louis regained his wits.

"All right." The concession cost her. He could see it as she swallowed her mutiny. She took his right arm, the warmth of her slender fingers burning through the sleeve of the jacket.

A breath of relief whooshed out of him and the stones crushing his heart eased up. She was safe. On his arm. They were leaving. Together.

He ignored the coat check line and regretted it as they stepped out into the icy air. Anya shivered in her next-to-nothing dress as the cold pebbled her skin. He shifted, yanking off his suit coat and draping it around her.

Fury kept the cold off. His car waited at the curb; the valet having taken the one hundred Swiss francs kept the engine running and waiting. Max opened her door himself and then passed another hundred to the valet. The younger man shot him a quick grin and retreated.

Right hand still bound in the napkin with ice, he shifted gears with care. He glanced at her in the shadow of the car as they lurched away from the curb and out into Geneva's nightlife. She remained uncharacteristically silent. He'd never been so glad to know a city as he was right now, putting kilometers between Louis and them.

"A ruble for your thoughts," he said after an expansive silence inflated the space between them to near unbreachable thickness.

"Did you get the Fortunate Buddha?"

"No."

She nodded but said nothing more.

"Anya."

"Yes?"

"Are you all right?"

Her startled glance flicked to him. He'd surprised her with the question. He tried to ignore the jerk of his heart. Why the hell is she surprised? He'd hardly masked his interest, much less the growth of his feelings.

Is she hiding hers?

"I'm-I'm fine." The stuttering response wasn't like her. He pressed the accelerator. He wanted to see her face. No, he needed to see her face. He needed to read the expressions rippling across it. The dancing shadows of streetlights and headlights left too much to the imagination. "Why didn't you?"

"Why didn't I what?" He swung through the palazzo and continued on to their hotel. He'd made arrangements for Pietr to move them after their unsuccessful attempt. Keep the ambassador guessing. Keep Louis guessing. Keep Anya guessing.

"What happened with Louis' system?" She didn't ask why he didn't retrieve the Buddha. She didn't point a finger. When he turned onto the Pont du Mont Blanc, Anya shifted. "Max—"

"Pietr moved us. I got past du Monde's fail-safes, but his vault utilizes a dual layer security system. Each is independent of the other except to deactivate one, you must activate the other. I made it through his external layer, but the internal is an inside job."

She sighed, the long, mournful sound etched with frustration. Max fingered the button at his collar and loosened it. His hand throbbed. He could wish he'd done enough damage to break Louis' face. His fingers clenched on the steering wheel. The image of Louis' head sweeping down to kiss her tore through him.

"I'm sorry." Her whisper punctured his haze of frustration.

"For what?"

"For not being able to get past the security, for walking in on Louis. I'm just sorry. I know it must be as frustrating for you as it is for me." She gave him another of those troubled looks.

Max tried to shrug, but the muscles bunching in his neck and shoulders prevented such a careless gesture. He couldn't just shrug it off. He hated the idea Louis ever knew the sweet temptation of her kisses or tasted the plumpness of her breasts or the sweet nectar of the juncture between her thighs. He couldn't stand the idea of Louis touching her at all.

The idea he'd been pawing her when Max walked in was just a visceral reminder they'd been down this road before. Louis had been her lover before. He could accept the idea in theory, but, in reality, it aroused a savage need in him to beat the man to a bloody pulp.

He wasn't quite sure whether it was because he didn't want her to recognize or want him or if it was just for the animalistic need to annihilate the competition.

Likely a combination of both.

"I'm not worried about it." How easily the lies rolled off his tongue. He could stomach the deceit if he focused on the job and not Louis. "Pietr and I will work out a method to get in and get out."

"That's a physical job."

"Oui?"

"You don't need to find anyone. I'm your grease man."

"Non." Finally across Lake Geneva, Max spared her a glance. "We will find another way."

"Other way? In a few hours? We're going to be lucky if Louis doesn't move it tonight."

"I don't care."

"I do."

Max's fist clenched, and he resisted the urge to pound it on the dash. Anya worked her way deep into his soul, pricking him whenever his thoughts turned elsewhere. Why couldn't she just understand he would do anything to protect her? Locking her inside an impregnable fortress, keeping the external security active so she couldn't escape, while she did the job wasn't an option.

No.

He might as well contact the authorities and just turn her in. It would be simpler than leaving her locked inside an artistic prison.

"I told you before you don't get to make this decision for me—"

He jerked the wheel, sending the car off the road and onto the slight shoulder. A forceful application of the brakes brought them to a sharp and abrupt halt. He twisted in the driver's seat and kissed her. He tasted the faint hint of her earlier drink.

It wasn't champagne.

He tasted none of the food he'd recalled on the table, only her sweet spice. A groan worked its way loose as she softened under his onslaught, tongue darting out to invite him. Her hands fisted in his shirt, and, if not for the stick shift jabbing him uncomfortably in his thigh, he'd jerk her over and take her here and now.

He exhaled the sweet flavor of her, letting her lips taste freedom as his forehead brushed hers. "You are impossible."

"It's part of my charm."

"If you wish to label it so." He grinned, and the anger burning a hole in his stomach ebbed. "I think you are a sorceress, entangling me in your spell until I can think of little else."

"Max, did you go to school to learn to say things like that?" Her eyes glittered with the passing lights, like captured stars across the sweet gray spring rain.

"Oui, an entire semester of romantic literature and passionate poetry."

She shuddered, and his smile grew. "A dangerous combination for a man like you."

"Merci, I think." He chuckled and kissed her again.

Long, heart-pounding moments passed as they touched, kissed, and held onto each other in the confines of the car. Reluctantly, Max withdrew. Her swollen lips drew him like a beacon.

"Do you have the schematics for Louis' place?"

"Oui."

"Then I just need to change, and we go tonight."

"Non. Dammit. I will not risk you."

And cold reality with isolated irritation doused their passion.

Max shrugged back into the seat, adjusting his seat belt and gunning the engine to leap out into traffic.

"It's not your risk to decide." Her voice echoed with patience, rationality, and the velvet steel of uncompromising determination.

She wasn't going to give up on the Buddha. It was the goal of their entire relationship. It opened the door, invited them in, and allowed them to savor each other for a while. They could abandon the quest. He would prefer it.

He would prefer no reason to end it.

He would prefer she wasn't so damn attached.

I'm a fool.

An hour later, she waited for the go ahead. They'd argued. They'd fought. But he'd finally acquiesced. She'd known he would. All charm and temper aside, he was a good man. He did the right thing. Getting the disc from Louis was as important as the Buddha. But if she failed to get the disc, the end of her IAAR relationship would be fait accompli.

The Buddha wasn't as negotiable. She wanted to complete the job. She wanted it returned to where it belonged. Louis deserved the icon as much as the French ambassador, which meant not at all.

"Pet." His whisper shivered through her ear and sent tingles radiating out of her belly. He spoke to her via a slender ear bud from two kilometers away. Need pulsed with each heartbeat over the way he said her name.

Looking upward, she inhaled through the nose for a count of four and then exhaled for the same count. She repeated it three times before her traitorous heart stopped keeping a mad cadence.

"I'm here," she murmured, aware the throat microphone, fitted to her like a choker, would transmit her words. She'd swapped out her dress for a black bodysuit, ropes, and microfiber gloves. They would reduce static, leave no prints, and still let her hands manipulate as needed.

Thankfully, he had most of the electronics on hand and found the other tools she needed.

"Stand by. I am checking on Louis' location and the status of the security." His tone assured her of competence, confidence, and calm. Not at all the man who'd argued with her all the way to the hotel in the car.

"I will not allow you to risk yourself!" His jaw clenched and his knuckles were white from gripping the steering wheel too hard. Even the knuckles on his injured hand began to weep with the quiet rage radiating off the man.

"It's not your risk to decide. It's my life. My freedom. My choice. You said we needed two people to get in there."

"Non. I said 'I' needed another, not you. Inside, you will be sealed within his electronic fortress until you have secured the items. The security information we have on the alarm system and physical threats...they are too sketchy."

"Well, it's a good thing I am trained and capable of such a task." She tried to keep her tone patient, burying the irritation of having to defend her own abilities.

"Why can you not understand I do not want you in danger? It makes me ill to believe I am the reason you are in danger in the first place...I am the reason you went into the theatre tonight and endured Louis' hands on you. I do not care if he was your lover before. I saw your face. I saw the revulsion. You would not have had to endure such a thing were it not for me." The agonized tone of a man being eviscerated slowly by his own guilt jerked painfully in her chest.

"Max...stop. I don't blame you. Yes, I was pissed. I was furious you put a camera there. But I'm not angry now. If you hadn't, well, I wouldn't have had this time with you, and I wouldn't trade it for anything and—"

"But—"

"No. Please. Stop. Let me finish." How could she not have seen his pain? He was such a light-hearted soul, so gregarious, charming, and sexy. Effortlessly so. But, it was the pain in him, the darkness eating away at his soul, shredding his joy, which punched her in the solar plexus.

That he could feel so agonized over her—for her—left her breathless.

"Oui, continue." He exhaled the words, finding the patience that just added to the pro list of his qualities.

"I am more than qualified to be the grease man. I know how to get in and around security systems. I'm limber. I'm small. I fit. With you backing me up, I know we can do this. Isn't it why you came to me in the first place, because you wanted to help? I want to help, too. This is my derriere hanging in the wind. I don't need you to save me. I need you to work with me."

He stared at her from across the dark of the car, his expression unreadable, but it was as though she could feel the weight of his regard boring through her.

"Oui. We will do it. Together."

"Thank you."

"Do not thank me yet."

"Pet." His voice dazzled her ears, and she forced herself to focus on the task at hand. The office building in front of her wasn't palatial, nor did it offer the suggestion of money. In fact, it looked like an ordinary office building one might find in any urban city location.

"I'm here."

"Good. I'm going to be deactivating the lawn sensors and front door cameras in thirty seconds. You'll have approximately fifteen seconds to get inside and across the lobby. I'm going to run the cascade failure in front of you. Are you still sure you want to do this?"

"You're so sexy when you're worried."

"Do not attempt to distract me."

"I didn't think it was an attempt." She grinned. She could picture the scowl rippling across his forehead and the fire leaping in his temper.

"Anya."

"Sir, yes, sir. Thirty second window. Fifteen seconds to get in and across the lobby to the second mark."

"Go."

She sprinted from her position on the rise, crossing the greenbelt with its snowcapped grass. Thankfully, the snow was light, or she would have been bogged down. Her boots slid on the concrete in front of the glass doors.

The lock popped easily. Too many security systems relied on their electronics. With their sensors disabled, the tumblers between the doors slid apart, allowing her to get inside. She spared two seconds to dry her damp feet before darting across the lobby, scanning for any manned security. Max said two were floaters located on the far side of the building. They wouldn't make rounds near the lobby for another three minutes.

Ideally, she wouldn't encounter anyone on her way in or her way out.

That was the plan.

But then, it was her plan with the Buddha the last time.

Now look at her.

"You're clear. Elevators are unlocking."

Chapter Eleven

"You have twenty seconds," he instructed after she left the elevator on the fifth floor. Louis' property included this fifth floor suite of offices. Nothing on the schematics described the interior. Internal and external security were intertwined. Internals could only be disabled if the externals were secured.

In other words, the office suite locked down like safe room. Her heart thumped a steady cadence as she strode down the hallway. Deactivating the cameras and lasers in the walls removed the only deterrent.

"Security has moved to the third floor. They will be arriving on the fifth in one minute." His tone was cool and detached, but his breath hissed with warmth and worry.

"Copy. I'm at the doors. Moment of truth."

"Once you're ready to open, I will cascade the systems on. The sensors and cameras nearest you will activate last. You need to clear the hallway and be inside before they reach you."

"Understood."

"It's an eight second window, Anya...."

"It's okay. Do it."

She gripped the door handle and braced her shoulder. The thud of her pulse drummed out other sounds. She concentrated on keeping her breathing slow and even. Her internal clock wound down the seconds, waiting for Max's go ahead.

The other side of the door was the gateway to her freedom. It could complete her work for the IAAR, and, while she would regret it if she couldn't work for them anymore, she would never have to feel like she let them down. Like she couldn't get the job done. The Fortunate Buddha would be returned to the temple where it belonged.

And what about you?

The pretty little liar in her head whispered the taunt, but she ignored it, and not just because she didn't have an answer for the question.

"On my mark," he murmured.

"Oui."

His chuckle cut off as the system whirred to life.

Eight seconds.

The cadence of mechanical clicks and hisses as the system cameras came online punctured the hall's silence.

Seven seconds.

She went to work on the door lock. Another basic office door with a dead bolt, but she had a key card reader.

Six seconds.

Numbers scrolled across the LED screen.

Five seconds.

The four-digit code appeared, one number at a time.

Three seconds.

Anya punched in the code.

Two seconds.

She swiped the card and turned the door handle.

One second.

She stepped inside and closed the door behind her, leaning against the oak.

"I'm inside," she murmured.

Max remained curiously silent.

"Max?"

She touched a gloved finger to her throat mic. She checked the ear bud, still in place. The room in front of her looked like an ordinary office lobby, with six or seven hard-backed chairs lining the walls, tables with magazines, and a dividing window which allowed the receptionist to closet herself away from the guests.

"Max?" She checked the microphone once more.

An electronic blanket must mask radio and wireless signals from leaving the room. No wonder he hadn't been able to access the secondary systems while the primary were operating. The primary were the electronic blanket.

She shook her head and focused.

She needed to find the disc and the Fortunate Buddha, not necessarily in that order.

His hand ached. His thigh burned. His jaw pulsed. Two minutes since she fell out of contact. Two interminably long, excruciating minutes of waiting. Blind, deaf, and mute, he couldn't warn her of any potential threats. He couldn't see what happened.

He couldn't hear her voice.

Fingers drumming on the laptop keyboard, he waited. They'd agreed on five minutes. They'd agreed, if for some reason they were cut off, they would give the other five minutes and then she would exit the office while he shut down the system to guide her out.

Five minutes was a reasonable period.

Five minutes was enough time to identify the Buddha's presence.

What can happen in five minutes?

Too much.

She checked her watch, two minutes in and no joy in the search. The office was a plain vanilla set up. She stood in the center of the reception room and turned in a circle. No art on the walls, except the one framed work of Lake Geneva opposite the frosted glass window of the receptionist.

The painting had beautiful detail, all watercolors and muted light. More Kinkade than Monet, with the focus blurred around grasses and trees in the distance. The rest of the office screamed ordinary, as if just waiting for the arrival of the same people to sit in the brown chairs, pushing their way through the hum-drum doldrums of life.

Why would Louis go to so much trouble to secure nothing?

Two-point-five minutes remained before her exit. If they lost communication, she exited on the five-minute mark. Period.

"With or without the Buddha, Anya. Get out of there." Max's order echoed in the back of her mind.

She planned for it to be with the Buddha.

Her attention returned to the painting.

Three-point-five minutes. Max's drumming fingers were picking up the pace. Not even the ache in his knuckles penetrated the stones piling up on his chest. Sweat beaded along his forehead. No job had ever been so tough. No security too tight. No anxiety so great he couldn't just shrug it off.

He hated to feel helpless.

131

She was alone, and all he could do was wait.

Not for the first time, he cursed the arrogance of his flat cam.

He'd just wanted a good look at her. He'd wanted to see her in action. He'd wanted to know how she did it.

Now, because he'd wanted to see, he was blind.

Four minutes and she swore. The safe behind the painting was so traditional, so cliché, so utterly, boringly normal, she'd cursed it. She could barely bring her breathing under control, head pressed firmly against the cool metal, listening. Her fingers turned the dial slowly, listening for the telltale click as it found the right number.

Safe cracking was IAAR 101—the most basic course. Their courses and training rivaled the highest-level locksmith school. Louis' piece of crap fell in the standard group: two combination locks with a flush dial. She recognized the make and model. They were placed between the studs in the wall with no protrusions. The flush placement with the art in front to conceal allowed for home marketing.

When she heard the second tumbler, she whistled out a breath. Sweat soaked her hair and made her catsuit uncomfortable. Less than forty-five seconds remained.

Breathe. Focus.

At the thirty-second mark, he queued up his logins and prepared to begin the cascade failure of the system. He'd been watching the security guards. They never exited the elevator on the fifth floor. They only opened the doors, examined the hallway, and moved down to the fourth to avoid triggering the sensors.

They were in the lobby. Their next sweep upward began in four minutes. They'd start on the lobby level and work their way up. The window between their movements would be narrow, but he could get her out. If it came down to it, he'd trigger every alarm in the building, create confusion, and allow her escape.

Fifteen seconds.

His heart pumped like a marathoner hitting the twelfth mile. Adrenaline sang through him. He didn't dare look too closely at his hands.

He knew they were shaking.

The safe popped open, and she stared. A sense of déjà vu flooded through her. The flat cam sat there, staring back at her, only this time sans the red light. Disconnected. A manila envelope with her name on it sat next to it.

But no Buddha.

Dammit.

She grabbed the flat cam and the manila envelope. Swiping her hand around inside the safe, she found nothing else.

The emptiness mocked her.

At the five minute mark, she eased open the door.

"Anya?" Max's voice, choked with emotion, thrummed past the heartbeat roaring in her ears.

"I'm here." I missed you. The chasm of five minutes seemed interminable. The manila envelope wasn't heavy, but the weight of it dragged at her. "Am I clear?"

"Head to the elevators. Take one to the third floor and hold."

"Okay."

"Are you all right?" He missed nothing.

"I'm good. The Buddha's not in the vault."

He swore, and she whispered the epithet with him. Exhilaration teetered toward exhaustion. She pressed herself flush to the wall of the elevator and waited.

"Forty-five seconds and they will begin their rounds. Hold."

"Okay."

She couldn't muster much more. Her vision tunneled, focusing on the round elevator buttons with their digits. The doors were open to the third floor. She barely remembered them shutting on the fifth or hitting the button for the third. Her brain fogged with the possibilities of the Buddha. Why had Louis secured the office?

Was it all a setup?

Had it been a setup from the start?

Were she and Max just the butt end of some cosmic joke?

"Anya?" His urgent whisper pressed past the sluggishness holding her hostage.

"What?"

"You're clear, darling. You need to move. We've only got about ninety seconds to get you down and out."

She hit the lobby button automatically and remained pressed to the wall so she wasn't immediately visible when the doors opened.

"Clear. Go."

His voice jolted her into a jog. She crossed the lobby swiftly, tucking the envelope and cam under her arm when she arrived at the door.

"Clear."

She pressed the handle, popping the doors open, dashed across the concrete forecourt, and headed for the snowy esplanade. The cold air struck her, sucking the oxygen from her lungs. The sweat on her body turned to icy chill. She shivered and her teeth chattered, but she kept moving.

Her boots slid on the snow, and she sat down to slide down the icy embankment right into Max's arms. They enclosed her like steel bands. She shuddered as foreign tears burned in her eyes and a sob clawed its way up from her throat.

He murmured in low French, his voice so husky and hoarse she could barely understand him. He guided her around the car and put her into the passenger seat before climbing in himself.

"Are you all right?"

"Fine." Not really. "Just tired." Scared. What the hell am I going to do now?

"Anya?"

"I'm sorry. The Buddha wasn't there." She couldn't look at him. She'd pushed for this. She'd pushed him into the hasty action tonight. She'd gone to Louis, letting him see her as she "distracted" him, and they still didn't have the Buddha.

"I don't care about the damn Buddha. Are you all right, luv?" There he was, the raw, deep-boned Brit stamping out the dark French seduction in his words. He split his attention between the road and Anya, but she didn't have anything else to say.

Another shiver racked her body, and he cranked up the temperature.

The cold dug into her flesh like needles filled with the poison of failure and fraud. She glanced at the flat cam and envelope in her lap. He hadn't even asked about them.

She wasn't sure she cared about them either.

Max stared at the closed bathroom door. Anya was slipping away from him. Sliding into the shadows of their shared existence. She'd been so silent on the drive, her shoulders slumped, her gaze distant. He'd tried to ask her about what happened, but she said very little.

He knew she'd wanted the Buddha.

But he hadn't imagined how crushing her disappointment would be when it wasn't there.

Nor how badly he would feel for her.

The vivacity, the sharp wit, and even the sly, sardonic smiles were gone for a pale, ghostlike woman who'd deposited the Judas flat cam and envelope in the middle of their bed before walking into the bathroom and locking herself in.

She hadn't said he wasn't welcome, but she'd not invited him either.

He looked at the envelope and the camera. He would take a hammer to the flat cam at the first opportunity. He wondered about the envelope until he flipped it over and saw it addressed to her.

Anya Foussard.

Her name.

The same name on her passport, but he hadn't expected it was real. No, she'd been too cagey about it, too reticent to share. So, why the name on the envelope?

Did she use the name before?

She'd found the items in Louis' office suite, but she'd said nothing about either one when she carried them into the car or when she'd dumped them on the bed.

So, what did they mean?

He reached for the envelope. He wanted to rip it open and see for himself, but he stayed his hand. The last time he'd wanted to see for himself....

He glared at the flat cam.

It brought her to him, and, now, it threatened to take her away. He shoved off the bed, stripping out of his clothes. He left them in a heap. The bathroom door wasn't locked, and the steam billowing out promised a scalding shower.

He didn't care.

"Max?" Her voice floated the question out on the steam.

"Oui. Expecting someone else?" He attempted a joke, but the words came out a growl.

She laughed, an unexpected gift.

Surprised, he pressed a hand to his chest to keep his heart from thudding free. He watched her through the frosted, multiple panes of glass. She stood, arms raised to the hot water streaming over her, her hair plastered to her skin.

She was a work of art in her own right.

"Do you mind if I join you?" He'd considered opening the door but hesitated. What if she didn't want him in there?

The glass door swung outward in invitation, and he exhaled through his teeth, slipping into the hot steam. His cock jerked to

135

attention as he slid an arm around her waist and drew her damp body to him. Her sweet vanilla scent beckoned beneath the layers of steam, shampoo, and soap. His heart gave his ribs a fist bump, desperation flooding his body with adrenaline and need. Burying his face at her throat, he inhaled a deep lusty, lungful, sating the immediate desperation to touch her again.

Now, he could take his time.

Anya sank into the plush pillows and slid her foot lazily up the back of his leg. He lay spent, cradled against her body. His hair was damp and tousled, the growth of five o'clock shadow matching the sadness she'd glimpsed earlier when he'd come into the shower. She'd expected him sooner but was still surprised when he did join her.

We failed. Why celebrate?

He kissed a path along her collarbone. His fingers stroked the line of her hip, and even his toes seemed to seek hers. His body buffered the last slivers of cold and shock clouding her mind. She'd never been quite so spectacularly unsuccessful before. A hard meal to digest.

"You're frowning." He stroked his fingers down the side of her face, and she turned to kiss his fingertips.

"I'm thinking about the Buddha. I'm wondering why it wasn't in the safe. What did Louis do with it? Has he already sold it?"

"I don't care." He shrugged.

"You don't?"

"I don't. I'm sorry it's gone. But I don't care enough to keep looking for it. To keep risking you...."

"I'm not ready to give up."

Disapproval shuttered him. His jaw tightened, stressing the hard planes of his face. "Anya."

"No, Max. You don't understand. I know you felt bad about the flat cam and you were worried about me—"

"Am worried," he interrupted. He shifted, rolling her over and pinning her to the bed, gazing at her steadily. "I am still worried. You found an envelope with your name on it. Foussard. Anya Foussard. I know it's not your name. I know it's just a passport you produced."

She swallowed the denial before it could trespass across her lips. It was a dropped ID. One of several maintained by the IAAR in secure lockboxes all over Europe and North Africa for just such emergency needs.

Getting the Buddha back qualified, in her opinion. She'd picked up the ID on their way to the airport, stopping at Barclay's. The bank offered private suites. She'd chosen the drop because she only needed a coded account number, a fingerprint, and, once inside the requested vault, a retina scan.

"It's not your name," he repeated.

Anya exhaled then nodded, her heart bruising for the tight lines around his mouth. She didn't want to feel bad about keeping her identity private. But she couldn't lie to herself. She couldn't tell herself it didn't matter.

"No. It's not."

He sighed and rolled away from her, sitting on the edge of the bed and reaching for his boxers. She extended her arm out, but he stood before her fingers brushed his spine. He strode across the room and picked up the envelope then helicoptered it across to land on the bed next to her.

"Is it the name you used with Louis?"

"No." She shook her head. "Max—"

"I don't want to hear about how long ago and what it was about. The thought of his hands on you—" He stopped himself from completing the thought. The muscles in his arms bunched and released as though the tension was a living thing, running along his body. "Just open it."

Dragging a hand through her hair, Anya sat up. The envelope mocked her. Her name staring at her in big, bold block letters.

Anya Foussard.

How the hell did Louis the bastard get that name?

He stood, arms folded, and moved across the room, the distance between them wider than the English Channel. Reluctantly, she ran a fingernail along the sealed lip of the envelope and tore it open.

When she tipped it upside down, a disc and a note fell out.

She looked at the disc and held it up to Max.

He nodded curtly. "It would have been in the flat cam."

The paper was simple white vellum, folded in half. Anya picked it up and flipped it open.

Ms. Foussard,

Viscount du Monde has been relieved of the Fortunate Buddha. My apologies I could not allow your paramour access earlier this evening, but I wanted to take advantage of the distraction you provided. I thought the disc might set things to rights between us. Please do forgive the disappointment.

Kit

"What?" Anya stared up at him. "This isn't from Louis."

He took the letter and scanned the contents. The tight lines on his face relaxed fractionally, laughter shaking his bare chest.

"This Buddha appears to be catnip to you thieves. None of you can keep your hands off of it."

Just like that, he lumped her in with all the rest—the hoodlums, the sneaks, the cat burglars. The fist squeezing her heart ground it, pumping all the feeling away until only a great gaping wound remained.

And why shouldn't he? You haven't told him the truth. You've held onto your secrets like they were one of a kind Versace dresses on a clearance rack.

"Well, it's over, then. Unless you have some idea who this Kit is, we're out."

"No." Even if she went to Walter empty-handed, pled mea culpa, and faced termination from the agency, it wasn't over. She'd find this Kit if it required spending the rest of her life looking for him or her. She'd find the Fortunate Buddha. She would return it. She would see the monks reunited with the idol.

Dammit!

She would return it.

"Is having the bloody thing worth so damn much to you? I could buy you a hundred others like it. I could drown you in Buddhas made from pure gold, platinum—whatever metal you want." Every word a slap. Her patient knight, her gentle lover, her proud partner in crime was done. It echoed in every sharp gesture and harsh word.

"Max, please—"

"Non. Enough. You can have your precious idol, or you can have me. What will it be?"

She gaped, but no sound escaped the vacuum in her heart.

He shook his head again. "I'm not going to beg. You have reduced me to a lot of things, but I will not beg you."

"I didn't ask you to." Where the pain went, anger ignited. She rose and took the sheet with her. All of a sudden, she didn't feel comfortable standing there with him staring at her, his disappointment and disgust evident.

"You're right. You did not ask." Max bowed his head, hands on his hips, and took several shallow, hard breaths. "We have the disc back. Your identity is secure. As for the rest...it will be handled. You have a way to return to London?"

Do I have a way...? He is leaving. Pain stabbed through the emptiness of her heart, gouging a path to her soul.

"Of course."

"Bon chance, then, upon your hunt, chérie." He dressed while he spoke, but he never looked at her. He strode to the door of the suite's bedroom, pausing to finally glance at her. Her heart ached for the loss of warmth in his expression, the emptiness in his tone. "The room is paid for the week. Help yourself to anything you would like. Thank you for letting me try to right what a wrong...." He seemed to think better of saying any more and turned the handle.

She wanted to call him. She wanted to leap off the bed and run after him. But the words wouldn't come, and all the reasons why she couldn't hammered away inside her skull.

Long after he was gone, she stared blindly at the opulence of the room. "My name is Anya Swift and I work for the International Art and Antiquities Recovery agency."

"My name is Anya Swift, and I'm not a thief."

"My name is Anya Swift...."

Too late.

He's gone.

"And I love you."

Chapter Twelve

One week later...

T he late January weather brought streams of rain pouring from the gray skies as though all of London mourned. Anya focused on the spaces between the rain. The minutia mattered very little, but it could preoccupy her thoughts. Not as though she were successful.

Nothing replaced thoughts of Max.

The car carried her to the gates of the IAAR and through them. It had arrived at her flat first thing in the morning with the summons. She would present her arguments to Walter and the oversight committee. They would then make a determination.

The best she could hope for was a six-month suspension of duties and referral to probation when she returned.

If they let me....

Walter had clearly told her to stay put, and she'd disobeyed his order. She'd not only left London, she'd traveled with Max to Geneva, burning one of her IDs in the process.

If she'd returned with the Fortunate Buddha, there might have been forgiveness following the scolding, and a future. The courtesy of a hearing surprised her. She smoothed a hand over the simple black skirt. She'd dressed in a suit for the less-than-festive occasion.

The gates rolled open at the car's approach. No challenge issued.

An oddity. But then she hadn't arrived in the back of Walter's personal transport before, and the two men in the front seat were more than adequately capable of vetting her. It wasn't like she was unescorted.

Neither man had spoken when they'd arrived at the flat. One

stood on the stoop with an umbrella while the other waited just inside. He'd taken her bag, examined the contents, and took the flat cam and disc into evidence. Max had left both behind in Geneva.

The car followed the tree-lined drive up to the main house then around to the rear where the carport would allow her to exit the car without getting soaked. Anya appreciated the thought.

Her escorts left her in a small sitting room with a fresh cup of tea and the stern advice to wait. She stirred the tea slowly, studying the paisley pattern on the wallpaper. Old school style, harkening to the days when the room might have been a more relaxing locale for the ladies following a meal. A long window overlooked the south lawn. But the steady thrum of rain bouncing on the grass and cobblestones added to the gloom.

"Anya." Walter stepped inside and shut the door. He waved her back into her seat when she started to stand. Dressed in a suit of dark charcoal gray, Walter creeped her out. She'd never seen him in such formal attire. His tie hung like a black-and-gray striped noose against the broad chest and darker gray of the silk shirt beneath it.

If not for the glimmer of sunshine in the form of a pale-yellow handkerchief poking out of his pocket, he'd dressed for a funeral.

Mine, perhaps?

She set the teacup aside and folded her hands in her lap. She'd once likened a summons from Walter to being sent to the principal's office. Despite the minor similarities, Walter was a great deal fiercer than the average principal. She interlocked her fingers together.

Walter sighed slowly and sat down across from her. His large frame looked awkward on the Edwardian sofa, but she ignored it.

"You've always been something of a maverick. Give me one good reason I shouldn't toss your ass out onto the fire where it belongs?"

"I have none. I didn't follow protocol. I disobeyed direct orders. I compromised a cover ID, and I wasn't successful in retrieving the Buddha. Twice."

"Twice." He nodded, his gimlet stare pinning hers. She wouldn't look away. Show the beast no fear. So, no to rolling over.

Not yet.

"As I said. Twice."

"So, no excuses. No martyrdom. No pleading."

"No, sir."

"Are you going to let this go? The Fortunate Buddha?"

"No, sir." She'd wrestled with the question all the way home from Geneva. Her answer already sent Max packing, so why change it now? She'd promised herself on the plane, in her flat, and in the car on the way to the IAAR.

The Fortunate Buddha would not be her one that got away.

"Bold. Direct." He leaned forward, clasping his hands together, and the brusque manner disassembled under the patriarchal mien softening it. "Headstrong and foolish. Sometimes it's better to just say done when it's done."

"It's not done. I was scooped. Doesn't make it done."

"Do you have a lead? Do you know where it is? Do you even know who the other thief is?"

"No, sir."

"Then it's done. The Fortunate Buddha is off the radar and out of our hands. Losing...losing isn't easy. It's not easy for the agents. It's not easy for the organization. But we have something on our side in this. Something that can make losing a little easier to swallow." The ice in his manner warmed a notch.

"We are many and spread out around the world?"

"No, Ms. Swift. It would be a terrible cliché, and, no matter how old-fashioned we might be, I've never been fond of the terrible cliché." Lady Amanda Prentiss knew how to make an entrance. Dressed in a pristine white dress suit, her coifed hair piled elegantly atop her head, she pinned Anya with her arresting green eyes.

Max's forest-green eyes.

His mother knows about the IAAR.... Does Max?

"As Walter was saying, Ms. Swift, we have time. This Kit who took the Fortunate Buddha. Maybe he or she stole it for him or herself. Maybe they stole it for a collector, maybe it will show up on auction, or maybe it will be buried in the bottom of a vault for the next fifty years. While unfortunate, it is of no matter because, sooner or later, it will come out into the light again, and the IAAR will be watching for it. We'll flag it, we'll tag it, and eventually, we will bag it." The woman's heels clicked decisively across the tile as she strolled into the room. Her unwavering regard held Anya hostage.

"But I'm the one who lost it." Lost the Buddha. Lost Max. Lost her heart.

"You were the agent assigned. No one can accuse you of not doing your due diligence. No one can accuse you of not risking yourself personally and professionally to get the job done. But you're not our first failure to retrieve. This is the hazard of the game we play. It's arrogant at best and narcissistic at worst to believe otherwise."

She'd read about verbal slaps in novels before; now she understood what was meant by the description. The candor of her delivery left no question in her mind about Lady Prentiss' opinion.

"Lady Prentiss...."

"Stop being a child. Jobs fail. Whether because of the choices you made or because of the choices of others, the result remains the same, the Buddha is out there. We do not have him in hand to return to our client today. But there is tomorrow and the day after and the day after that. If you make this your personal crusade, you're going to get drummed out of here faster than you can add a jot of sugar to your tea."

"You mean I'm not out now?" Her composure evaporated under the heated admonition in her voice. Hope flared in her chest, easing past the trapdoors of guilt and grief.

"No. You're not out now. You're going to be on probation for a while and the council has determined oversight will watch your assignments a little closer for the time being, but what's done is done. No matter how tough the situation was or how badly it might reflect on you, you've been clear in your reports and you never compromised the agency—"

The image of her out there hadn't endangered the IAAR—only her. "No, ma'am, I did not." *Even though I wanted to. Even though if your son waited just a few seconds more, I might have squeezed those words out.*

"Your actions reflect the strength of character we first admired in you. Beyond your skills, your talents, and your abilities."

"Walter?" Anya glanced at her mentor. Wasn't Walter the one who picked her out? Hadn't he ferreted her on a job?

"Surprised you, eh?" His broad, craggy face broke into a grin.

"I thought my ability earned your notice and the fact you saw me on the job."

"Oh, it might have been what caught our notice, earned you a more thorough look than a glance, but Lady Prentiss admired your character, your determination, and your honor."

A wry laugh twisted her lips. *Moral honor.*

A master thief with honor among other thieves. Though more privateer than pirate at their core, they remained thieves. Max's accusation still stung and remained nearly impossible to refute. And even now, the pain of it left welts on her heart.

"You scoff, but it's there. It's likely what attracted my son to you. Are you two going to be seeing each other regularly, now?" Lady Prentiss folded her arms, the casual note barely disguising the marble tone beneath.

"Um, no." Humiliation rushed to flame her face.

"Why not?" Was his mother seriously asking her this?

"He washed his hands of the situation and me."

"Really?" Lady Prentiss arched a delicately plucked brow. "He met with the French ambassador in Rabat two days ago."

Fear sliced through her.

"Is he all right?" Why Max? Why? Why? Why in all the great why world of whys would you go there? He threatened to kill you.

He threatened to kill me, too.

Anya ignored the niggling little voice, uncrossing her legs and edging forward on the seat to lean toward the pair. She studied their faces, looking for a nuance of expression or clue to reveal Max's fate. He had to be okay. She couldn't imagine his mother would be this cool if he weren't.

"He was fine when his flight left Rabat this morning. He transferred about thirty million pounds from a private account to the ambassador."

Anya tried to control her reactions, but her emotions collided too quickly, too furiously to be reined in, even with a breathing exercise. Max paid off the ambassador.

"Did it occur to you the reason my son paid the ambassador was for the Buddha?"

The question slammed a concrete block in front of her runaway emotions. The shock, so fierce and taut, actually struck her like a physical blow, robbing her of breath and speech.

"What?" She shot to her feet.

Lady Prentiss shrugged. "Thirty million is hardly pocket change. I doubt he paid for the privilege of the New Year's Eve party. Unless the party favor in question was the Buddha."

"No." Flat. Absolute. Denial.

"You can't be sure...." The woman made a show of checking her diamond-encrusted watch.

What the hell is wrong with you? She swallowed the hostility. She didn't know what game they were playing, but Max wasn't involved. Not like that. He wasn't the liar, she was. She was the one who hadn't told him the truth. She was the one who'd used the excuse of the Buddha and the flat cam to get close to him. He'd at least confessed his sin.

She'd just stayed quiet.

Not anymore.

"Yes, I can." Her spine stiffened, and all the confusing cacophony of questions tumbling inside of her stilled into one pure voice. "He planted the flat cam for personal reasons. He's not a thief. He's not dealing in stolen property."

He is innocent.

"But you can't be sure and, if he did play you, using your attraction to get to you...you're a beautiful woman with many, many talents. Or so I am given to understand."

Judgmental, dismissive witch.

"I can be sure. And if you knew your son, you would be sure, too. That's not him."

"You spent, what, a week with him? Do you really think you know my son better than I do?"

"Why? Because I'm not filthy rich or privileged? Because I don't have a pedigree attached to my name? He's a good man. I don't care what you think you know about him, I know Max didn't take the Buddha. I know he wasn't paying the ambassador for it...." Her mind raced.

"Unless?" Lady Prentiss prompted.

She shook her head. There was one reason Max might have paid the money. But it seemed so much, and he'd been so angry. "He isn't the reason the Fortunate Buddha is missing."

"You believe in him so much?" Although he didn't move from the sofa, Walter's tone changed, a subtle challenge threading through each syllable.

Max's hand on her nape....

His fingers brushing down her cheek....

The way Max smiled as he kissed her....

The raw ache in his eyes when she refused to give up the search....

Anya lifted her chin and met Lady Prentiss' gaze unflinchingly even as she answered Walter's question. "I do."

"All right, then. We'll monitor the situation, but we won't move on it. Not without some evidence of the Buddha cropping up."

"Understood."

"But you're still going to look for it." It wasn't a question.

Anya's lips flirted with a smile, barely tipping upward as she looked at her friend and mentor. She wouldn't lie to him. She wouldn't even attempt it.

Walter scratched a brow with one finger, seemingly studying the wall beyond her. "Very well, you're on vacation for the next six months. I'll expect you to report in directly on the first of July. We'll review available assignments then."

"I'm suspended."

"No, vacation, Ms. Swift," Lady Prentiss interjected. "You've worked for us for six years. Consider it a month of leave for each year of your employment. Take care of this, Walter. I have phone calls to make." The woman turned to leave the room.

"Wait." She took a step forward, blurting the word out before she could stop herself.

"Yes?" The arctic would offer a warmer reception. The noblewoman waited.

"Does Max know about the IAAR?"

Lady Prentiss tipped her head to the side. "Why do you care?"

"Just...it doesn't matter why I care. I just want to know if he knows." Her stomach cramped. Had he known about the organization all along? If she'd been able to confess all of it...could they have avoided all of this mess?

"No, Ms. Swift. He doesn't. At least not yet. Walter. Ms. Swift." Lady Prentiss didn't wait for any further comments.

Anya watched her leave, dread curdling in her belly. "So, I didn't do anything wrong, but I still get punished."

"You were compromised. You've put your reputation and your career on the line. You've been through the wringer emotionally, and you're still dealing with the fallout. Not every affair is the love story of a lifetime, but you should grieve at least a little when they end. I think you're grieving a lot, and you're looking at work as a substitute. You know it's not acceptable here." Walter's gruff tone held very little sympathy.

She did know, but she needed the investment. She couldn't let go of the Buddha. If not for it, her soul wouldn't be shredded right now.

"Six months. You finished your degree. You'll still draw your monthly stipend. Travel. Have some fun and relax. Maybe get out of London and go somewhere sunny and warm." Walter stood, and Anya joined him, accepting his offered hand. He gripped her gently, the squeeze unexpected as it was welcome. "Majorca is lovely this time of year, as are Cancun and the Virgin Islands."

"Thanks Walter, but...."

"Sauvage has a house on Majorca, though, so you might want to add the island to your travel plan considerations."

She blinked. Was there a hint of a twinkle in his eyes? "I think I can take care of myself, Walter."

"I don't doubt it. Six months. Not a minute sooner. And if you come across the Buddha between now and then...."

"I'll call you in six months."

"Good girl."

She smiled and then hugged him. It was a strange impulse, one she'd never experienced before. Walter was stiff at first, but then he embraced her and ruffled her hair with a halfhearted pat.

"Be good to yourself and take the vacation." He kissed her forehead before walking her toward the door and the car waiting out in the rain.

Anya began to smile.

Six months.

She could do a lot in six months.

***

Max poured himself another drink and walked to the double-wide doors facing the blue sea beyond. Majorca was lovely this time of year. But the sun, the sand, and the wide sprawling house on the lip of the island did little to lift his bleak and bitter mood.

"We should call those girls from the bar yesterday. They are in port for just a couple of days. The blonde-haired one...she liked you." Pietr spoke from the lounge chair where he sprawled, sunglasses hiding his expression. He wore white cotton britches and no shirt. His bare feet were as bronze as the rest of him.

Pietr really favored Majorca and had spent a week trying to cajole him into a game, a bet, or a job which would earn him the property. Unfortunately for his cousin, Max wasn't in the mood.

"Invite who you like to the hotel. I don't really want them here." He took a sip of the amber liquid. The bourbon was not his first choice, but the burn eased the ice coating the inside of his chest, allowing him the illusion of warmth penetrating the cloud of disappointment clinging to him.

"Maxwell." Pietr spread his arms wide. "This is not healthy for you. You spend all your time here, alone."

"I'm not alone," he responded drily.

"Without a woman, Cousin. A woman to play and ponder with in this paradise. It's not meant for the lonely-hearted who dull the white sands to something gray and brittle even as the sun dims, saddened by your countenance."

He paused to look over his shoulder and snorted. "Pietr, the hotels are just a few kilometers down the beach. Go find yourself a pretty girl and enjoy."

"But how is a man to enjoy himself if he knows his cousin is here, alone, in the middle of the day, drowning his manhood in bourbon." Pietr motioned to the splashing waves beyond. "Paradise has no place for pain. Purge it with the pleasure the island has to offer."

He sighed and shook his head. Pietr had been the same for days, spending hours nagging at him to go out, to eat, to change, and, now it seemed, finding a woman had joined his to-do list. "Did you forget to pay off a credit marker somewhere and lose your soul to my nursemaid?"

"Non. But you are not yourself. It makes me sad to see you this way."

"And you don't like to be sad." Max's mouth twisted into a wry smile as he washed down the rest of the drink.

"Exactement! But all you do is mope, drink, and mope some more. I thought there would be some excitement when you took the jet to Rabat, but you returned even more drunk and stinking than when you left."

"I showered."

"Only after I threatened you with the soap bucket."

Despite himself, he laughed. The chuckle rumbled past the hurt, scratching its way through the solemn miasma surrounding one stormy image in his mind.

"It's been difficult for you, Pietr."

"Oui."

"You don't have to stay."

"But what kind of a cousin would I be to abandon you in your time of need?"

He decided not to answer.

"But you could make it up to me?"

He grinned, but he didn't turn and reveal the expression. "How much would it cost me?"

"A few hours of your time, more or less...."

"I'm listening."

Chapter Thirteen

Rain-flavored breezes pulsed in the ocean air. Max leaned against the bar, contemplating swapping to beer for the novelty of it. Pietr wanted to throw a party. Not just any party, but a carnival replete with feathered masks, ball gowns, and men dressed in stockings and powdered wigs.

It was ridiculous.

But it was exactly the kind of ridiculousness he needed. He'd been brooding for a week. Brooding since he stormed out of the Noga Hilton in Geneva and driven to the airport and boarded his jet. His pilot had already been moving them out onto the runway when he'd had his change of heart.

But he'd been too late.

She was gone. She'd taken the flat cam, the letter, and left only the sweet citrusy scent of her femininity as a reminder. Calls to the airport and local transportation earned him nothing. Anya Foussard didn't exist. She wasn't leaving Geneva. No, she would have left under another name. He'd toyed with the idea of Anya Sauvage, but it proved an empty bubble.

He should never have pressed her.

It was an idiotic moment borne of masculine pride and ego. The Fortunate Buddha brought them together, but it was he, not the Buddha, which drove them apart.

He had no one to blame but himself.

"Maxwell!" Pietr strode across the party, his Phantom of the Opera mask giving him a rakish air.

"I don't think they heard you on the balcony. Perhaps you'd like to bellow louder."

Pietr smirked at him. "Cousin, you wound me. But you should know I do not take it personally, and I am here to put you out of your misery."

"Isn't that what this is all about?" He gestured to dozens occupying the gaming tables and makeshift dance floor. Pietr must have spent thousands to turn their Majorcan beach manor into a bordello of debauchery and midnight madness.

His cousin slung an arm around Max's shoulders and leaned in conspiratorially close. "I'm tired of your brooding. You're boring this way."

"Sorry to disappoint." Although his tone denied any sincerity.

Pietr grinned. "She's not a thief, thief, Max."

"What?" His focus sharpened, as though yanked through the filmy curtain keeping him in a stupor.

"Your Anya. She's not a thief, thief. You haven't been yourself since Geneva—well, truth be told, since Rabat—but I put it off to the madness of lust. After Geneva, I was not so sure."

"Pietr." He straightened, shrugging off his cousin's arm. "Get to the point."

"She works for the IAAR."

"The what?"

"International Art and Antiquities Recovery."

"The foundation tracing the genealogy of artifacts. Mother is on their committee...or she was."

"She still is." Pietr grinned. "I called darling Aunt Amanda when I kept running into dead ends in her Foussard backstop ID." Pietr's grin grew, but Max ignored the pride in his voice, trying to latch onto the details.

"So, you called my mother?"

"Aunt Amanda is well-connected, and she called me three days ago and asked for a copy of the images we have of her."

"My mother knows her." He tried to wrap his mind around the idea Lady Prentiss and Anya were acquainted and served on some committee. An ache formed behind his left temple. "What does the IAAR have to do with...?"

Pietr watched him with interest. "Recovery is the key phrase in their title. They are a foundation on the surface. They do research and establish the genealogy of items, tracing ownership over generations. But they also restore artifacts and art pieces illegally obtained to their rightful owners."

He frowned. The noise of the party faded around them as laughter and music scored through the room. He tried to wrap his mind around the idea his mother was party to an organization engaging in illegal activities. It was vaguely shocking.

Of course, he wasn't above the occasional creative interpretation of the law.

"Max." Pietr snapped his fingers in front of his face. "Your mother gave me Anya's name."

Hope flared amongst the dusty ashes of his heart. Her name.

Her real name.

He could find her.

She wasn't a thief.

That wasn't important.

"Name. Now." He shoved his drink aside and was already pushing his way across the crowded deck. If he called the pilot on the way to the airfield, he could be in London in a few hours. She lived in London. Most likely near the little shop in Hammersmith. The knowledge narrowed his search considerably.

He could be face to face with her by tomorrow.

"Where are we going?" Pietr asked.

"We aren't going anywhere. I am. Call the airfield; tell Jason to have the plane fueled and on the tarmac. We're flying to London. Then call Rockston at the London offices." Max glanced at his watch impatiently. "He's probably in bed but wake him up. I need an address." He cut a glance at Pietr and paused. His cousin was wearing a wide grin.

"I told your mother you were in love. It was the only way Aunty Amanda would play."

"I am glad my romantic status pleases you."

"Oh, well, oui, but I just won a year with a yacht in the Mediterranean. She told me I was wrong."

Laughter jolted through him, a low-throaty laugh centered somewhere around the base of his spine that sent electricity humming through his muscles. He forgot about Pietr, his mother, the yacht, and looked around the crowd of people.

He knew that laugh.

The partying sounds, music, and even the wash of the water against the beaches below the house drifted away as she walked out the doors of the main house. The carnival mask with its peacock feathers and rich hues of blue and green hid her face, but he recognized her body. Her sweet, warm-toned body sheathed in a black silk dress caressing every curve as she walked. The slit in her dress played peek-a-boo with a length of bare, tanned leg.

His body jerked as he roared to life.

"Max, you're not—"

"Pietr."

"Oui?"

"Go away."

Pietr's grin faded to a frown until he followed Max's gaze. Max ignored Pietr. He ignored the party. He followed the line of her legs, legs he knew so well, legs that ended in a pair of red strappy heels.

Anya's heart boxed her ribcage with a solid one-two cadence. She held the clutch purse tighter in her hand, trying to control the quivering. When she'd arrived at Heathrow yesterday morning, she'd fully intended to purchase a ticket for the States. She was going to go home to Minnesota, to her normal parents in their normal house on their normal suburban street and let normalcy be a salve for her wounded heart.

But, standing at the ticketing counter, she'd asked about Majorca.

Then she'd bought a ticket.

Something Walter said niggled in her mind. Walter knew her. She sometimes thought he knew her better than she knew herself. The summons, the drive out to the IAAR estate, the meeting in the tearoom—it had all been to talk about Max.

He'd planted the seed about Majorca. He'd brought up Max, the Buddha, the payment to the ambassador, and she knew Max had only done it to keep the ambassador's goons from hunting her down.

She'd known it as surely as she'd known black Prada and Versace was a match made in the Parisian fashion halls. He'd protected her. He'd been furious with her. He'd washed his hands of her. He'd left her.

But he was still protecting her.

She told herself over and over again she didn't need anyone's protection, but the warm glow pooled in her belly and spread throughout her body as the thought of his actions brought home why some women swooned.

She wanted to swoon.

If her muscles hadn't locked, she would have swooned.

He was worth swooning over.

Discovering his estate on Majorca was hardly a trial. She'd planned to break in, sneak into his bedroom, and seduce him, but the party was the talk of the town. Never one to turn down an opportunity, she relied on the familiar—now lucky—dress and purchased a mask in her hotel's gift shop.

Standing on the deck as twilight rushed to embrace the day, she found her heart's frenetic beat left her breathless. All around her, couples danced, played, laughed, and chattered. But she hunted for only one pair of forest-green eyes.

The crowd swayed and moved, an entity unto itself, parting ever so briefly and revealing him, not ten meters away, his attention riveted on her.

Her lips cooled and tightened as all the moisture fled her body under the scorch of his gaze. She drank in the sight of him.

He looked good.

His hair blew in the evening breeze. His white cotton shirt was open to his breastbone, revealing the dark tan of his skin. A white linen jacket gave his casual appearance the look of careful choice while enhancing the rakish appearance of his strong jaw, dark hair—gorgeous, gorgeous man.

Her legs rooted to the spot. She needed to start walking. She needed to cross the deck and walk to him, but her body refused to listen. Inside, a riot of emotions collided and exploded like the fireworks illuminating their first night of passion.

Max said something to the man at his elbow and strode toward her. Behind the mask, she smiled. He was coming.

He was coming to her.

In four precious seconds, he stood in front of her.

"Chérie," he whispered. Awe and something sounding a great deal like affection mingled with longing in his voice.

"Max."

With a tentative hand, all the more endearing for its hesitation, he reached up to tug off the mask, and she let it fall away. The week behind them stretched out like an endless, bleak pit of nothingness. Standing on the far side of the hellish separation, she recognized it wasn't the Buddha or her job or her honor that mattered.

Max mattered.

"Would you care to dance?" He didn't wait for her to answer. He swept her into his arms and turned her into the dancing couples, twirling her, dancing along to the current of music, his body brushing hers. Hunger sang through every nerve. Her body ached for him.

It took everything she had not to kiss him.

"How are you?" he murmured, each word whispering his breath across his skin.

"Better. So much better. You?" Pleasure eddied through her muscles as her body dipped and swayed, his arm held her close, and the fabric of her dress did nothing to mask the hard, hot heat of him.

"I am also better." He smiled, and her heart stuttered. "It is an unexpected pleasure to find you here."

"Is it?"

"Oh, very much so."

"So, you were still looking for me?" Hope caught her up and flattened its fingers over her spine.

"Always." The fierceness of his declaration arched her up onto her toes.

"You didn't give up?" It was her turn to sound awed. "You left."

"I came back. You were gone."

"I thought you were leaving me."

"I was an idiot."

"No, I was stubborn."

"You were honest. You didn't try to make promises you didn't think you could keep. I was being selfish."

"No, you weren't." She looked into the haunted forest-green begging her to throw caution to the wolves and explore. "You have been nothing but generous. You didn't have to warn me. You didn't have to hunt me down in London. You didn't have to help me go after Louis. You did all of it for me. I was just...my training, my job. I couldn't tell you anything more."

"Anya, shh. You should know, chérie, I never give up. I never will. And I will never walk out again. I will protect you. I will protect your secrets. I will never demand you choose between me and your honor again." They were away from the partygoers, in the shadow of his house, with a full and pregnant moon rising over the water.

"But you don't know all my secrets." She'd rehearsed her speech on the plane. She'd rehearsed the words. "I'm not a thief, not a real one. Well, yes, a real one, but I work for a good organization. A great one, in fact. They reunite lost artifacts with the rightful owners." She was so making a mess of this.

"I know you're not a thief, and I don't care about your secrets or your IAAR. I just care about you."

"I'm so sorry." She caught his face in her hands and leaned up, meeting his kiss halfway and thrilling to the way he plundered her. Her arms twined around his neck, and he lifted her, holding her to him, tongue darting in and tasting.

"I've missed you," he groaned.

"I missed you, Max, wait." She willed him to look at her. His face was flushed, relaxed and a twinkle sparkled in the depths of his eyes, like fairies in a forest. She was going there. "I need to tell you I'm sorry I wasn't truthful with you, and I do want to tell you my name—"

He paused and pressed a finger to her lips. "I don't care what your name was."

"Was? No, I mean what my name really is," she murmured when he swooped in to steal another kiss, swiping her thoughts with it. He nibbled kisses along her cheek to her earlobe and then tugged it gently.

"Night jasmine and oranges," he whispered next to her ear, warm breath sending shivers dancing up and down to her toes. "Anya, I don't care what your name was or has been. I only care what it will be."

"Will be?" She frowned as he pulled away, fingers trailing down her arms to catch her hands in his. Still holding her attention, he descended to one knee. The ocean breeze caught her whispered oh and tossed it out to sea. The world stopped, as though holding her breath in anticipation.

"I promise I love you and trust you and honor you and will for the rest of my life if you would do me the very great honor of becoming Anya Sauvage for now and always."

She swallowed. The tears that threatened to storm earlier, fell. "I love you. I really love you. You scared me to death. You were everything I ever imagined I could want, and I thought I must be mad to want it so badly. I thought if I acted like it was just an affair, my heart wouldn't be broken, but you've had my heart for so long I think it forgot it was mine to begin with."

His expression softened, his smile growing, but he remained on one knee. Waiting.

"There is so much about me you still don't know...."

"And I will have a lifetime to discover it all. Say yes, Anya. Say yes, mi amour, and we will spend our lives finding every hidden treasure you've ever dreamed of."

"I don't need to hunt for treasure anymore, Max. I found the most priceless treasure of all." Her heart swelled, thumping hard, so eager to be with the man it had given itself to so long ago. "Yes, Max. I'll marry you."

He grinned and surged upward, catching her in his arms and kissing her. Beyond them the partygoers roared in approval, applauding the couple who never broke from their kiss as the first firework illuminated the sky.

Anya Sauvage.

His.

Now.

Forever.

About the Author

National bestselling author, Heather Long, likes long walks in the park, science fiction, superheroes, Marines, and men who aren't douche bags. Her books are filled with heroes and heroines tangled in romance as hot as Texas summertime. From paranormal historical westerns to contemporary military romance, Heather might switch genres, but one thing is true in all of her stories--her characters drive the books. When she's not wrangling her menagerie of animals, she devotes her time to family and friends she considers family. She believes if you like your heroes so real you could lick the grit off their chest, and your heroines so likable, you're sure you've been friends with women just like them, you'll enjoy her worlds as much as she does.

Also by Heather Long

Always a Marine
Series so Far (in order by release)

Once Her Man, Always Her Man
Luke & Rebecca

Retreat Hell! She Just Got Here
Logan, Jazz & Zach

Tell It to the Marine
James & Lauren
Introduction of Matt McCall and Damon Sinclair
Features an appearance of Logan Cavanaugh

Proud to Serve Her
Damon & Helena
Matt, James, Lauren, Luke and Rebecca mentioned

Her Marine
Brody & Shannon

No Regrets, No Surrender
Logan, Jazz & Zach
James featured

The Marine Cowboy
A.J. & Sheri
Phone call from Luke

The Two and the Proud
Rowdy & Kim

A Marine and a Gentleman
Brenden & Liam
Appearances of James, Logan, Jazz, Shannon, Rebecca, Lauren

Combat Barbie
Kyle & Mary
Jazz makes an appearance via phone

Whiskey Tango Foxtrot
Joe & Melody
James makes an appearance

What Part of Marine Don't You Understand?
Matt & Naomi
Appearances by James and Logan, Damon is mentioned

A Marine Affair
Eli & Rick

Marine Ever After
Paul & Lillianna
Multiple appearances at Luke & Rebecca's wedding

Marine in the Wind
Greg & Georgia
Appearances by A.J. & Sheri

Marine with Benefits
Derek & Kara
Appearance by Logan

A Marine of Plenty
Charlie & Jana
Appearance by Naomi

A Candle for a Marine
Isaac & Zehava
Appearances by Zach & Shannon

Marine Under the Mistletoe
Kaiden & Rowan

Have Yourself a Marine Christmas
Rebel & Noel
Appearances by Derek, Kara, Luke and James

Lest Old Marines Be Forgot

Tom & Brenda
Appearances by Luke, James, Logan, and Damon

Her Marine Bodyguard
Shannon & Brody
Multiple appearances including Luke, Logan, Zach, Jazz, Mary,
Damon & Rowdy

ROAR Series

Mischief, Mongrels & Mayhem

The Black Hills Wolves

What a Wolf Wants
Wolf in Winter Clothing
Scent of Madness

The Love Thieves

Catch Me
Hunt Me
Treasure Me